"I'd prefer to [...] you"

"Why?"

"Because you've been sweet to everyone else and I want you to be sweet to me."

Daniella was slightly taken aback by how bold and direct he was. "How?"

He moved closer. "Kiss me."

"Is that an order?" she teased, stalling to make sure she was ready to take the leap that was before her.

"I could make it one. But I hope I don't have to."

Daniella recognized the challenge more because of his intense, smoldering gaze than by his tone, although she had to admit that was just as inviting. She leaned forward, ready to fulfill his demand on her terms. "All right," she said then touched his lips with hers, wanting to give him a quick, indifferent kiss. But he didn't give her the chance. The moment their lips touched a rush of emotions assailed her body, and his arms circled her waist and brought her close. He pulled back a moment and stared at her in wonder. "It's amazing."

"What?" she breathed, equally in awe.

"You actually taste as sweet as you look."

DARA GIRARD

fell in love with storytelling at an early age. Her romance writing career happened by chance when she discovered the power of a happy ending. She is an award-winning author whose novels are known for their sense of humor, interesting plot twists and witty dialogue. When she's not writing, she enjoys spring mornings and autumn afternoons, French pastries, dancing to the latest hits and long drives. Dara loves to hear from her readers. You can reach her at contactdara@daragirard.com or P.O. Box 10345, Silver Spring, MD 20914.

A Reluctant
HERO

DARA GIRARD

HARLEQUIN®

entertain, enrich, inspire™

To my devoted fans.
Your support means more than you know.

Recycling programs
for this product may
not exist in your area.

ISBN-13: 978-0-373-86282-5

A RELUCTANT HERO

Copyright © 2012 by Sade Odubiyi

www.Harlequin.com

Printed in U.S.A.

Dear Reader,

I first introduced the Duvall Sisters—vain Mariella, kind but plain Isabella, sweet Gabriella and innocent Daniella—in *The Glass Slipper Project*. They later popped up in *Taming Mariella*. When I took a break from the series, I received emails inquiring about the remaining sisters.

"Are you going to write more about the Duvall sisters?"

"Will we ever get to find out what happened to Daniella?"

"What about Daniella? Will she finally get her own story?"

At last, here's your answer. Daniella Duvall may still be considered the baby of the family, but as Trenton Sheppard will soon find out, she's all woman and ready to heal his broken heart.

If you're new to the Duvall sisters, welcome. And if you're coming back, I hope it's a reunion you won't soon forget.

Enjoy,

Dara Girard

Chapter 1

It took Daniella Duvall approximately ten minutes to realize that the man she'd convinced herself she was in love with was actually a jerk. But she let this new information settle slowly in her mind as she watched him from across the elegant restaurant table with its cream tablecloth, fine china and gleaming cutlery. The long-stemmed rose that sat on the table between them, looking elegant in an Austrian glass vase, suddenly seemed like a mockery of romance. She thought of throwing his glass of red wine in his face and watching the residue drip on his gray silk shirt. Daniella thought of slapping him, but that would be too cliché and could get messy. Besides, he would probably file assault charges against her. She thought of just getting up and walking away, but that wouldn't faze him. He'd expect her to come back. Women always came back to Pascal Bordeaux. She had to admit she was one of them; she was his ex but still in his life because he was a brilliant man to know.

During the time she'd been dating him, Daniella had learned a lot about him. She knew he'd been born Parry Baines in a small town somewhere in Georgia and because of a speech impediment had had extensive speech therapy to correct it. In college, he'd used a dialect coach to help him rid himself of his strong Southern accent, making it have a more mainstream cadence. He'd studied the famous actor, Sidney Poitier, who grew up in the Bahamas and had a thick island accent. When he had his first byline article printed in the prestigious University of Pittsburgh's magazine, he'd chosen a new name for himself that wasn't mainstream at all. Soon it became more than a pen name, it developed into a new identity, forcing him to fudge certain aspects of his past, such as his parentage and background, to make his name more plausible. Now he'd risen too high for anyone to refute his ownership of a French-sounding name, and his new identity suited him. He was an author and professor at the local liberal arts college.

What she didn't know was how lucky Pascal had felt to have found her and now he hoped to rekindle what had been lost. She'd fit perfectly into the life he'd created for himself and the image he wanted to maintain. And he enjoyed showing her off in public. Just like her two other sisters, she had inherited the Duvall stately beauty—elegant neck, dark flashing brown eyes and skin the color of polished oak. He loved how her long, curly hair looked when she smoothed it into a French roll and the color that filled her cheeks when she was riled.

No, Daniella didn't know any of this and likely wouldn't have cared. Instead she watched his mouth move and set her knife and fork down trying to keep her voice from trembling once she regained the ability to speak.

"Cute? You think my article was cute? You invited me here to tell me that my story was cute?"

He reached across the table, covered her hand with his and smiled, an effective and practiced smile, to calm her. His eyes were warm and concerned, tinged with a hint of regret. "Dani, I wanted to see you and what I said I mean in the best possible way."

Daniella wanted to scream, but she drew her hand away and kept her voice level. "In the best way? How is that possible? You read my article describing my harrowing journey surviving a plane crash and you thought it was *cute?*" She flexed her hand, taking control of her temper. She'd made a mistake in coming to see him. Why did he always put her down? And why did she let him? Why did she care?

Pascal glanced around the room as though embarrassed that their conversation could be overheard, although in truth no one was paying attention. "There's no need to get upset."

"Too bad because I *am* very upset. I'm furious!"

Pascal sat back and smoothed out the napkin on his lap in a quick, restless motion. "Why are you making such a big deal out of this? It's not like it's high journalism. It's just your regular work. You're a talented writer," he said, his tone just shy of patronizing. There was an element of sincerity that kept Daniella seated instead of walking out the door.

"Just not as good as you, right?" Daniella said, annoyed that she still craved and delighted in any crumbs of praise he sent her. It was because she admired him so much. She was still in awe of his Pulitzer Prize winning article about urban street kids being forced into slavery, by being "bought" by wealthy residents in a major U.S. city. He'd turned it into a book and a film documentary produced by *Frontline,* a highly respected TV show on PBS. She'd met him years ago while attending a journalism convention in Niagara Falls and instantly felt an attraction. Aside from being very handsome, eloquent and stylish, he was interested in the same issues she was. But she broke up with him when she realized he didn't see them as equals. And now as she stared at him across the table she saw that nothing had changed. She had worked hard on her article, hoping it would catapult her stagnant career to the next level, but he'd dismissed her efforts and with it her entire writing career as just fluff.

Daniella tapped the table. "This article isn't like the rest. I share the experience of eight other passengers and—"

"And it's good work."

She gritted her teeth, his indulgent tone beginning to grate on her nerves. "But you could have done better," Daniella finished in a flat tone. His words hurt, although she didn't want them to. He'd touched her deepest insecurity. That he was right—they'd never be equals.

He shrugged. "I didn't say that."

"You didn't have to."

Pascal took a sip of his wine and flashed another one of his soothing smiles. "Let's change the subject."

"No, this is getting too interesting." She pushed her plate aside and leaned forward, resting her arms on the table. No matter how harsh his words, she was ready to face them. She was determined to get her career to a level where she garnered the same respect he had. "Tell me what you would have done differently."

He sighed, resigned. "You're not going to like my response."

"I don't care, tell me anyway." She lied, knowing that she would care, but ready to accept what he had to say.

He sighed again as if he knew he'd regret his next words, but continued anyway. "First, I wouldn't have done a story about my experience." He held up his hand before she could argue. "I would have done a story on the pilot."

"The pilot died. He suffered a heart attack. It would be tragic to tell his story and cruel to his widow."

Pascal brushed her words away with a wave of his hand. "Not him. I mean the guy who rescued the plane. The one who you said jumped into the cockpit and took over and helped all of you to survive for four days in the wild." He pointed at her. "Now that's a story. It was staring you right in the face and you missed it."

Daniella blinked. "But that's not my story."

Pascal shook his head and flashed a sad smile. "The problem with you is that you just don't have the instincts. You had the perfect angle to launch your career into the stratosphere and you let it slip through your fingers."

"I knew other reporters would beat me to it," Daniella said in her defense, hating how close to the truth she knew he was. "They were swarming all over the guy when we were finally rescued."

"He's still a mystery. He won't talk to anyone. It appears as if his background is as bland as mud."

"See?"

"Yet you were with him for four days. Do you know how much you can get to know about a person in that amount of time? There are memories locked in your mind about that man and the event that people would pay for."

"I wasn't the only passenger."

"But I can bet you were the only writer. You're trained to be observant. You probably know a fact that no one else does. You may have noticed something that could tell us more about him."

"But—"

Pascal raised his hand. "No buts and no more excuses. They're all flimsy anyway. You should have done a human interest story on Richard Eagle."

"Correction, it's Engleright," she said.

"Right. If you'd done a story on him, that would have been impressive. I mean where was he trained? Why did he walk away? Why won't he talk about the accident? There's a gold mine of a story there."

He was right, there was a story there and she'd missed it. Pascal had always been able to see the right angle for any story. She didn't. She'd convinced herself that it was because after being with Richard Engleright for four days she'd wanted to forget about him. She hadn't been able to yet, but she would. Daniella focused on her food, but she saw Richard's face. Richard by the creek, Richard by the fire, Richard kissing her... No she wouldn't think about that. It meant nothing. She stabbed her asparagus. She'd seen and learned a lot about the man but thought he had the right to keep his secrets. She wasn't a writer who dug for dirt.

"You missed a great opportunity, Dani, but that's okay. We both know that it's out of your league."

Daniella's head shot up. "No, it's not."

He laughed. "Dani, this guy is good. There's no way you'll be able to get his story when professionals can't."

"I am a professional."

"A professional travel writer, you write about luxury hotels or hot vacation spots. This is different. You'd have to find him, convince him to talk to you and—"

"I can do it," she said, ready to meet his challenge.

He cupped her hand in his, his voice soft. "I'm sorry I hurt your feelings. Your story is really good and great for your portfolio."

"But it's not good enough."

He frowned. "Stop putting words in my mouth."

"Then stop talking to me as if I was one of your students."

"I'm just being honest."

"I'm going to get his story."

Pascal began to grin. "I'd like to see you try."

Daniella bit into her asparagus, mentally hoping that getting Richard's story didn't mean she had bitten off more than she could chew. But she was determined to wipe the smug grin from Pascal's face.

"Are you out of your mind?"

"He said my story was cute!"

Sophia Carlton, Daniella's best friend from childhood, and roommate, stared at her bewildered. They'd been instant friends and become even closer after Sophia's brother, Alex, married Daniella's sister, Isabella. Usually, as good friends, they bragged about being able to read each other's thoughts. This wasn't one of those times. They both sat in the living room of their stylish apartment—or rather what passed for stylish in the small town of Hydale, New York. They'd briefly lived in the city, but the cost was too much and the pace too fast. So they returned to their hometown close to their family where Sophia worked as a grants manager for a high-tech company. Daniella could always count on Sophia to be her support…until now.

Sophia waved her finger. "I don't care if he said it was bubblegum, that doesn't mean you should try to find this stranger and write a story about him."

"I'm going to show Pascal what I'm really made of."

"You don't even know where to begin."

"Yes, I do."

Sophia folded her arms. "Fine. What are you going to do first?"

Daniella glanced out the window. It had been two days since her talk with Pascal and she still didn't know where to begin. "I haven't put my plan together yet."

"See? You're out of your element."

Daniella turned to her. "I can't believe you're taking Pascal's side on this."

"I'm not taking sides." She threw up her hands. "I can't believe you don't see how he's setting you up for a great big fall. Nobody's been able to get this guy's story."

"I can."

"How?"

"I'll find a way." And she would. She'd show them never to underestimate her again. Daniella could just imagine their faces when she showed them the printed article. Editors would pursue her for more stories, and maybe she'd even be offered a six-figure book deal. She began to grin, picturing Pascal's shocked expression as she signed her books in front of a large audience of fans and...

"Don't do it."

Sophia's words cut through Daniella's daydream. She frowned at her friend. "Do what?"

"Whatever you're thinking about."

"You make me sound devious."

"Because you can be. Everyone thinks you're sweet and innocent, but I know you better than that."

Daniella sighed. Sophia certainly did. Growing up together and traveling as adults, the friends knew the "true" nature of one another. Most people paid little attention to Daniella because she looked young and naive. It had once been an advantage, but now had become a hindrance because people didn't always take her seriously.

"This is my chance to show the world who I really am," Daniella said.

"You mean Pascal. You're doing all this because of him."

Daniella tilted her head to the side and studied her friend. "You never liked him."

It was a rhetorical comment, but Sophia answered anyway. "No. I think he's a pompous ass and just as fake as his name."

"I told you that in confidence."

"It doesn't matter anyway. Now you feel the same way I do, right?"

"Yes...no...I don't know." She sighed.

Sophia groaned, exasperated. "You're not sure? Only two days ago you came home telling me how awful he was and how you were going to 'show him.' Now you're telling me he's great again?"

"I'm not saying Pascal's great, but he's right. If I were really a storyteller I would have thought about doing Richard's story instead of mine."

"Your story was great. It was featured in two national magazines. That's excellent and the money was definitely real." She touched the new blouse Daniella had bought her to celebrate.

"That night you said I should go for it."

"Because I thought you were just talking. I was being supportive. I thought it was just bravado, I didn't think you meant it. Now, days later, in the cold light of day you're telling me you're planning to track down a mystery man who could be a fugitive hiding from the law for all we know."

"Even though we officially broke up, we're still friends."

"Sure," Sophia said, unconvinced.

Daniella tucked her feet underneath her and sunk back into the couch. "And I see him as a mentor."

Sophia rolled her eyes. "Perfect. As if the guy didn't need his ego stroked anymore, you still worship him."

Daniella folded her arms. "I don't worship him and any criticism he gives me is because he's pushing me to be better."

"He's a jerk," Sophia said, not wanting to pretend anymore.

"No, he's forcing me to stretch myself," Daniella said, warming to the subject and hoping her words would give her the courage she needed to start. "He's right. I should try to get the story that no one else has. I've stayed too safe." She sat up straighter and tapped her chest. "If anyone can get Richard's story I can. I was with him long enough to figure out certain things about him."

"Daniella, this is a really bad idea."

"I have to do this. Not just to prove it to Pascal or you but to myself."

Sophia sat down beside her friend and held her hands. "You don't need to prove anything. Especially not to me. You're an extremely successful travel writer. And you live well and have a good life."

Daniella chewed her lower lip. "Ever since Pascal brought up Richard's name, I just can't stop thinking about him."

"Pascal?"

"No, Richard."

"Try."

"I have tried."

"Try harder."

Daniella laughed. "I can't try any harder. He's like an itch I have to scratch."

"You need to let *someone* else write the story."

"No. I want it to be me."

Sophia shook her head. "You need a break. Go to a spa, or go soak in a nice Jacuzzi."

"But—"

"Forget him."

Daniella knew she couldn't, at least not that easily. After Pascal had given her the challenge, the man from the crash had filled her thoughts. She hadn't been thinking about him, now every moment he seemed to rise in her thoughts and she couldn't forget anything about the day he had come into her world. How could she forget the man who'd saved her life?

Chapter 2

Four months earlier

She was alive. She didn't know how long it had been since the moment of impact—it seemed like hours, days—but her pounding heart let her know that life-supporting blood was pumping through her veins. That the sound of torn metal and the ominous groan of the plane settling between the trees was over. There had been screams, now everything was strangely quiet.

Daniella raised her head and chips of shattered bonded glass and plastic material used for airliner cabin windows rained down from her hair, shoulders and back and dropped to the ground with a tinkling sound. The smell of wet earth invaded her nostrils. Their trip had started off as a routine flight from Nova Scotia. That morning she'd been running late and was one of the last passengers to board, so she'd been able to see everyone else. There weren't many of them so it was easy to remember them all. She'd seen two brothers teasing each other throughout the flight. From their conversation she knew they had come back from visiting family. They were both redheads who could have passed for identical twins if one didn't have a mustache and a heavier build. He'd winked at her when she'd asked for help with her bag. Next she'd seen an older woman with bleached blond hair, carefully applied makeup and tight, pinched lips that made her face look like she'd just smelled something foul. The fourth passenger, a young woman beside her, was also a blonde, but naturally so. Everything about her was fair, from her hair, lashes, eyebrows and skin. The black shirt she wore gave her skin an eerie, translucent look as though if the sun's rays were to hit her directly she would completely disappear. It was clear from the way they interacted that the poor girl knew the older woman. She was a companion or relative of some sort, Daniella didn't know which. There was the tall, thin man with large glasses that made his eyes small and then lastly, the two children, around eight or nine, with honey-brown hair, neatly dressed and oddly quiet.

The first person she'd noticed on the flight, but the last to come to mind, was the man she'd dubbed The Renegade. He had a cool lonerlike quality and while they had been waiting to board the plane he stood off to the side away from the crowd. He didn't look like the sort that would fit in or would want to. He looked more like a man who'd likely look good in jeans and leather (preferably black) but he wore neither. Instead he wore dark trousers and a suede jacket. Daniella had first noticed him when she had offered a smile that was either rebuffed or ignored. She was slightly disappointed when she was seated beside him, because she would have preferred a more friendly companion, but she was glad it would be a short flight.

Daniella remembered the sound of laughter and easy chatter before the weather change, and soon the mood of the passengers did, as well.

The pilot's voice came booming through the plane's speakers. "Make sure your seat belts are buckled. We're heading into a storm so there will be some turbulence."

It felt like more than turbulence. Suddenly, Daniella felt as if she was on a ship being tossed by large waves in the sea—the plane was rocking to and fro and up and down. One moment they were experiencing smooth flying then they plummeted several feet before the plane settled again. No one spoke. Tension and fear hung as thick as the dark clouds that surrounded them. The overhead lights came on in the cabin, but only emphasized the blackness that enveloped them. Daniella had looked out the window but there had been no point, it was like looking into a pot of thick pea soup and she hoped the pilot's visibility was better than her own. She looked at The Renegade, but knew he'd be no source of comfort. He was alert, not panicked but on guard as if he sensed something wasn't right. But she'd flown through storms before, Daniella knew they'd be okay. She considered making a joke, but soon thought better of it. Instead she focused on the article she had to write about her recent trip to Nova Scotia, Canada, and the notes she had to clean up for her editor. She took a deep breath. They'd get through this.

Without warning the plane took a sudden nosedive. Screams filled the air and the man beside her rushed to his feet and disappeared into the cockpit. She went into the emergency position she'd learned from the many flight drills she'd practiced and thought of her family. Then her mind went blank.

Daniella still couldn't remember the impact or how long she'd been hovering with her hands over her head. She knew one emergency had been averted, but they weren't out of danger yet. Now there was the sound of rain and she felt the cool of the approaching evening. She noticed that a thick tree branch had gone through one of the plane's windows just behind her. Seeing how large the branch was and how close it was to her head, she was surprised and relieved to discover that no one had been decapitated. Tree branches mingled in a macabre arrangement with the plane's brightly colored orange cloth seats. She decided to look around to check on the other passengers.

She turned and saw the older woman with the pinched lips frantically tugging at her seat belt. "No, no, you're doing it wrong. You imbecile!" she said to her companion. "I bet you'd like to leave me here to die."

"No, Mrs. Pruit," the blonde woman said in a weary voice.

Daniella recognized her tone. Her elder sister Isabella had had to work for a similarly demanding woman and she'd also had to play that same role for a while. She knew the other woman needed help.

Daniella stood, then grabbed a seat to keep from falling because the plane leaned at a strange angle. Once she had regained her balance she made her way over to the older woman and her aide and said in a calm voice, "Come, let me help you."

"I don't need help," Mrs. Pruit snapped. She pointed an accusatory finger at the younger woman. "She's the one doing it all wrong."

Daniella shrugged. "Well, if that's the case I'll just leave you." She turned.

"No," the woman said in a voice of panic. "You…I—girl, come back here!"

Daniella sent the young woman a look of sympathy then unlatched the seat belt and helped the older woman out. Then she started to count heads. She remembered the boisterous brothers who were sitting toward the front. Those seats were empty and the emergency chute deployed so they must have made it out safely. She'd just helped the older woman and her companion and both looked in good shape, with a few bumps and scratches. She was glad to see the thin young man with large glasses and a mustache who had sat behind her was also gone. Lastly, there were the two children. She walked down the aisle and found them crouched between the seats, holding each other.

Daniella reached out her hand to them. She knew that in a crisis some people ran while others froze. "Come on," she said in a gentle voice. "We have to go."

"I'm frightened," the girl said.

"Anna won't leave and I can't leave without her," the boy said.

"You don't need to be frightened anymore, we're safe on the ground. Come on."

She kept her hand outstretched and slowly the children stood and followed her. Once they were safely out of the plane, Daniella did one last check and then walked into the cockpit and bit back a scream—three men lay slumped over. She walked over to the pilot on the floor, but from the color of his skin she knew he was dead and had been for a while. She'd seen death up close before and knew what it looked like. But she still felt for a pulse. Nothing. Next she went to check the copilot and sighed when she felt his pulse. It was faint but it was still there. He was alive. She jumped when she heard a strange noise. She turned and noticed that the last man was watching her. It was The Renegade. His eyes were like petrified wood—hard, sleek yet bright with pain. But instead of making him seem vulnerable, he appeared more watchful, assessing. Daniella suddenly became acutely aware of his brute strength, keen intelligence and piercing gaze. An intensive shiver slid down her spine. He was a man to approach with caution. She walked over to assist him but he held out his hand keeping her away.

"What are you still doing in here?"

"I'm here to help," she said.

"Where are the men?"

"Everyone got off safely. I made sure."

His jaw tensed. "You did? Did they help you?"

"No, but—"

"Three healthy men left you to take care of the rest of

us?" he said with disgust. "Is that the new modern man? Leave the woman and children to fend for themselves?"

"I'm sure—"

"The pilot's dead," he interrupted, obviously in no mood for excuses.

Daniella paused. "I know. What happened?"

"Heart attack most likely. It was quick, the impact didn't kill him."

"And the copilot?"

The Renegade briefly shut his eyes. "He likely has a concussion."

"But how? Didn't he take over when the pilot had his attack?"

"No."

"Then who landed the plane if...?"

"Let's just say my flying lessons paid off." The man grimaced, but remained silent. Daniella sensed there was something he wasn't telling her but now wasn't the time to press him.

"What about you?" she said, quickly looking over him for any major injuries. "What's wrong?" she noticed him rubbing the upper part of his arm.

"Old injury. I'll be fine in a minute."

"We need to get out of here in case the plane explodes. That's probably why the others left." Daniella's voice betrayed her calm demeanor—she didn't want to get blown up.

"Honey, if you were worried about that you should have been gone long ago."

Honey? "I'm trying to help."

"I know. Relax. It's not going to explode."

"How do you know?"

The Renegade sent her a measured look. "It would have done so by now. Do you really think I'd be lying here if I thought it was going to burst into flames?"

He had a point, but she didn't like his attitude, treating her as if she were some hysterical female.

"What's your name?" he asked in a curt tone.

"Daniella."

"Richard." He slowly rose. "I knew I should have taken the train."

"Are you trying to be funny?"

"No, I *am* being funny."

"Then you have a sick sense of humor."

"True, but laughter makes the world go round."

"No, that's love."

"If that were true, the world would have stopped spinning centuries ago." He gestured to the copilot. "Help me with him."

Daniella helped The Renegade grab the copilot by each arm and slowly pulled him out. His name was Herman Walker and he was a veteran pilot, owing to the fact that he'd worked for Canadian Airlines for over twenty-five years. He kept drifting in and out of consciousness. They set him down near a tree and Richard assessed his injuries then nodded and stood. "We'll have to watch him but he'll live." He glanced at the airplane, which looked like it had survived some sort of bomb attack. From the look of the damage Daniella knew they were all lucky. She was alive. She looked at Richard again. His expression remained guarded, it seemed he was used to emergency and disaster. Now she was safe. Everyone was safe because of this unexpected hero. She looked at him once more, telling herself that she was just curious about him, but knowing instinctively that her interest in him was much more than that. He had a magnetic presence and her eyes soaked up his broad shoulders and powerful frame. He stood as if he could take on the world. The camera was going to love him. He was not typically handsome. The word handsome would be too ordinary a term to describe him and he was far from that. He had a rigid jaw that hinted at a stubborn streak, but it was softened by a mouth that shouldn't have been so enticing. It should have been a hard mouth to match his eyes. But instead his lips were soft and she could imagine them melting into a smile. She felt her skin tingle at the thought; he seemed like the kind of man who could put his mouth to good use beyond just a sexy smile. But that didn't matter because he wasn't her type. Men like Pascal—refined, engaging, charming—were her type. Not hard, cynical men like him.

"What really happened?"

Daniella expected him to pause or hesitate as he came up with a suitable lie to soothe her, but he did neither, he just continued to stare at the plane as if Daniella hadn't spoken.

"What happened?" she asked again, insistent.

"I told you what happened." He rested his hands on his hips, broadening his shoulders. Daniella fought not to notice. "Or rather what I think happened."

"You explained what happened to the pilot, but not

the copilot. How could he have lost such control of the plane?"

He shook his head. "You ask the wrong questions."

"What should I be asking?"

"How are we going to survive until help arrives."

"But I want to know what happened. Why did you end up having to fly the plane?"

Richard turned to her, his eyes like obsidian orbs. "It was a freak accident, leave it at that."

Daniella folded her arms, unafraid but rather more intrigued by him. "You know something."

"I know lots of things. None of which I plan to share with you right now."

Before heading toward the plane, Richard took several minutes to check on the other passengers. Surprisingly, everyone escaped basically unscathed except for a few bruises. He stood and started to walk to the plane. Daniella began to follow.

"Stay here with the women and children," he said. "I need to talk to the men." Before she could argue he pointed at the two brothers and the tall thin man. "You guys, come with me."

They looked at each other, but didn't move.

His tone remained soft but became more ominous. "Unless you want me to shame you in front of these women you'd better follow me now."

They did. He led them close to the plane, but not inside.

"What do you think they're saying?" the little girl Anna said, still holding her brother's hand.

"I don't know," the young woman said.

"What did they do?" Anna asked, her voice shaking with fear and almost pleading.

"Something really bad," her brother said. "He doesn't look happy."

That was true. Although his hands remained rested on his hips in what could have been a casual stance, Richard looked like a leader in front of his platoon. The fury that emanated from him was clearly visible and as he spoke the men seemed to get smaller and smaller. Moments later they returned with their heads bowed.

"Since we're going to spend some extra time together," Richard said, clearly taking the lead, "I think we should introduce ourselves."

Introductions were made. Wendell Scottsdale was the tall, thin man. He was an insurance salesman. Glenda Travis Pruit was the unfortunate daughter-in-law to Mrs. Mavis Pruit. At present her only profession appeared to be that of being nursemaid, but she had once been crowned Miss Georgia before marrying Mrs. Pruit's son. Stephen and James Baxter were brothers who lived in upstate New York where they ran their family business, making small parts for military planes. Lastly, there were the two children, Anna and Mark Thompson, who were traveling alone to go and live with their great-aunt after losing both their parents in a recent car accident. While the children had not been forthcoming in telling everyone their fate, Daniella was able to pry the truth from Anna, and could understand why they had been abnormally quiet throughout the trip.

For a moment Daniella was angry. Why hadn't anyone accompanied them on the trip? Especially after going through something so traumatic as losing their parents? Someone should have taken the time to be with them instead of them traveling alone. But now was not the time for her to be concerned about something she could do nothing about. The last person to introduce himself was Richard.

"My name is Richard Engleright and the main thing you need to know about me is that I have training in survival, and if we work together we should be able to survive until we are rescued. Wendell, you and Stephen can go and gather what food and bags you can salvage from the plane." Richard looked at James, the heavier of the two brothers. "Help me bury the pilot."

"No," Daniella shouted. "I think we should wait until we're rescued."

Richard spun around and looked at her surprised. "What?"

"Do you have to do that now?"

He lifted a brow. "Are you expecting a priest or rabbi to show up?"

"You really have a terrible sense of humor."

"I'm not trying to be funny."

"We can't bury him here. What if his family wants to bury him?"

"They can do that later."

"Why don't we just put a blanket over him?"

Richard's eyebrows shot up. "A blanket? Maybe we should just tuck him to sleep and say 'Rest in Peace'?" He held up a hand before she could protest. "We're burying him because we don't want him exposed to the elements or, even worse, a coyote, fox or bear. I'm not leaving a dead man out like that. You're going to stay near the center of the camp and—"

"I don't take orders—"

"Then you'll start now."

Daniella rested a hand on her hip. "Listen, here—"

"No, you listen to me. I'm in charge and you *will* take orders from me."

"You're the leader?" she sniffed. "Was there an election I missed?"

"The moment I took over the plane I took office. I claimed leadership."

"Well, I think—"

"No," he cut in. "This isn't a time to think. This is a time to follow orders. To trust that your leader—that's me—will make the best decision for all of us. This is not a meeting of consensus. From the way we landed and the damage, I know that the plane will never get off the ground, or trust me, I'd try to fly us all out of here. I know how to survive and I'll make sure that you do, too. Is that clear?"

Daniella took a deep breath, biting back what she really wanted to say. She understood his taking control. It couldn't be a democracy where they voted on every point. Instead, it was a hierarchy and he was the alpha male as much as she hated to admit it.

"Is that clear?" he repeated.

Daniella offered him a mock salute. "Yes, sir."

He flashed a cool smile, as if reluctantly offering her a salute, recognizing them as equals. "I'm glad to see you have a sense of humor. Now take the children to gather wood, but don't wander off too far."

Daniella could feel everyone looking at her. Tension lingered and she knew only she could ease it. She took one of the children's hands. "Okay."

"Gather wood? What for?" Mrs. Pruit said. "You mean we have to stay out here?"

Richard sent her a cool look. "If you know of more luxurious accommodations, please feel free to lead the way, madam," he said with a broad mocking gesture.

"Is that a joke?"

"It's whatever you want it to be."

"Shouldn't we try to see if there's a town or city nearby?" Glenda asked.

"No. Besides, we need to stay near the plane so it will make the rescuers' job easier to find us. Think of it as an unexpected camping trip."

"I hate camping," Mrs. Pruit said. She tried to use her cell phone then tossed it down in the dirt in disgust. "You could have at least had the foresight to land the plane in a clearing where we could get a wireless signal."

"I'll remember that next time." He walked away.

All of them, including Richard, had tried using whatever electronic equipment they had to see if they could get a signal and call out, but because of where the plane had landed, their efforts were futile.

"Without a signal how will they find us?" Wendell asked.

"The plane has a transmitter. It shouldn't take them too long to track us." Richard knew he needed to smother any mounting anxiety, although he was totally convinced that the transmitter wasn't working. He just hoped it was.

"Are you sure they're looking?"

"Yes. Now that's enough talking, daylight won't last forever. Let's get to work." Richard looked at the copilot, who was still resting over to the side, and knew that he needed to find some kind of shelter immediately if his condition wasn't to get worse. He had been checking on him every fifteen minutes, and while he had fully regained consciousness, he didn't remember anything about the accident and had suffered a slight ankle sprain and a pulled shoulder muscle. Richard had administered some first aid, and recommended total rest.

Daniella helped the children gather wood and once she was done she sat, or rather collapsed against a tree feeling strangely light-headed, but she attributed it to the shock of everything—the crash, the dead pilot, The Renegade. She just needed to rest. She drew up her leg and lowered her head. When she looked down she saw fresh blood. That's when the pain hit. She slowly pulled up her trouser leg and saw a large gash. She glanced around, glad that everyone was too busy to notice her. She didn't want anyone to see and worry about her. They all had to be strong. She didn't want to be the weakest link.

"What's wrong?"

She froze, recognizing the voice and hearing the demand in it. The tone didn't anger her because she could hear the concern he was trying to hide under his brusque tone. She bit her lip, hoping to take control of her racing heart. She looked up at Richard then jumped to her feet not wanting to draw any attention to her wound. She'd tend to it later. "Just have to catch my breath. Do you need me to do something?"

His keen eyes searched her face. "Sit down." He shook his head. "Please don't argue with me."

She sat. "I was just taking a quick rest."

"Are you hurt?"

"I'm fine."

"Then why is your face pale?"

"How do you know?"

"I can tell by looking at your lips."

"I'm looking this way because I just survived a plane crash."

His hard eyes studied her and then he looked down and swore. Fresh blood soaked through her trousers.

A flash of emotion crossed his face—a mixture of anger and regret. He hung his head for a moment then looked at her again, his eyes no longer hard, but amazingly tender. "Damn, I checked everyone except you. I just assumed you were okay." He turned away and swore. When his gaze returned to hers, the distant mask had settled back in place—all softness gone. "Why didn't you tell me about this?"

"I didn't know about it until now. I hadn't felt it."

"Too busy trying to be damn Florence Nightingale," he grumbled. He stood. "Wait here."

Daniella gave him another mock salute. "Yes, sir."

He hesitated then left. Moments later, Richard returned with water and a first aid kit. He pulled out a knife and cut away her trousers, revealing a large wound. He swore again, this time with more emotion.

"You should have told me or someone. Do you think it will help any of us if you get sick out here?"

"I told you that I didn't know. I didn't feel anything until now. It's not like I did it on purpose and I'm fine really."

"You're not fine. You're already running a fever," he said, holding the back of his hand against her forehead. He applied some peroxide to the wound.

Daniella felt the world spinning and her stomach turn over. "You're not allowed to faint," he said.

She steeled herself against his harsh words. "I wasn't going to."

"Good. You're strong. I need you to stay that way."

She would. She didn't want anything to do with this hard uncaring man. No, that wasn't fair. He could be caring. Although his eyes could be like chips of ice, she'd seen moments when they'd briefly melted and in turn could have melted her heart if she let them. There was another side of him that a part of her wanted to uncover and another part wanted to remain hidden. He was a man who knew a lot about the world and would fight to get whatever he wanted from it. She could just imagine how he'd be if the right woman came into his sight. How would he act if he wanted a woman? She could picture him using his magnetic command, a dark glance to hypnotize a woman to abandon any wariness she may have and surrender. But that woman wasn't her. She needed to focus on survival and nothing else. Richard's movements were surprisingly swift and efficient. Her wound looked bad, but he didn't make her feel bad about it. He had done it before and she was grateful for his knowledge, wishing he wasn't so disagreeable.

"I had to do it," he suddenly said as if reading her thoughts about him.

"What?"

"At the camp. I had to establish my authority. I couldn't have you fighting me at this critical point."

"You didn't have to challenge me so publicly," she said, glad he'd brought up the topic. "You could have pulled me aside—"

"No, I had to let everyone know where I stood and where you and I stood. The fact that we work as a unit had to be established and made clear."

"You certainly did that, sir."

"My name is Richard."

"Does it matter?"

"Yes, that's what I want you to call me."

"Another order?" Daniella scoffed.

Richard's eyes pierced hers and for a moment she felt as if she couldn't breathe, or didn't dare to. "You don't have to like me," he said. "It would be easier if you did, but it's not important. I need to know you're loyal to me. You're my second-in-command."

"A promotion? I'm all aflutter."

He finished bandaging her leg and sat back. "Sarcasm doesn't suit you."

"Sorry, sir."

He grabbed her arm, his face close to hers, his voice low. "You don't seem to understand the risk you're taking." His gaze dropped to her lips. "You're a powerful woman."

Daniella swallowed hard and licked her lips, trying not to tremble. He would feel it and part of her wanted him to. She forced a laugh. "Me? Powerful?"

"Yes, you." His gaze held hers. "You don't fool me. I can tell you've got a lot of strength."

She stared back in shock, mesmerized by his dark eyes. Perhaps he'd hit his head harder than she'd thought. No one had ever thought of her as strong. Her sister Mariella, yes, even Izzy and Gabby, but not her.

"People will follow you," he continued. "You can influence others. If you cause any break within this group our chances of coming out of this alive will plummet. Do you understand me? I don't care if you like me, just act cordial and do your job."

"And obey you?"

"Yes. Now say my name."

Daniella's heart picked up its pace, aware of how close they were. "Sir."

His gaze again fell to her mouth and lingered there, as tangible as a caress, making her lips tingle. "I knew you'd be trouble."

She began to smile, wondering how far she could push him, but when his dark, unfathomable eyes captured hers she realized she couldn't push him too far without dealing with the consequences and she wasn't sure she was ready for that. She knew that in an instant he could turn from prey into predator. His lips always made her forget that. They really didn't seem to suit the rest of him and they were her biggest weakness—seeming so soft and inviting. She forced her gaze to his eyes. She had expected them to be as hard and unrelenting as before, but instead his eyes were like melted brown sugar and she saw the glimmer of a slight plea there. She knew this wasn't a time to play games. He had to know he could trust her, but right now he was unsure and she knew that he wanted this to work. He knew the dangers they faced and she couldn't be another obstacle for him. She had to think of the others. "Yes, Richard."

He released his grip and stood. "Good."

"Sir," she said under her breath as a sly comeback.

"I heard that," he said, with a smile in his voice, as he walked away. The remainder of the day was spent retrieving whatever they could from the plane's cargo hold. There was an emergency kit that contained essential items needed to survive several days, including waterproof and windproof survival blankets that would reflect up to ninety percent of their body heat. It also included a butcher knife, sharpening stone, lightweight LED flashlights, waterproof matches, a compass, metal cup, signal mirror and water-purifying tablets. In a separate section of the plane, they were able to locate a medium-sized cooler loaded with nonperishable items, primarily canned beans and tuna fish, and several jars of peanut butter. Richard knew that they would be able to survive at least for several days, but wasn't sure what he'd do after that. He just hoped they would be found before he had to face having to make that decision.

Richard was a born leader. He instructed the Baxter brothers to clear a section of earth near the plane, so that they could use the body of the plane to provide shelter from the elements when the temperature began dropping in the evening and through the night. Next he instructed Wendell and Glenda to start a fire once Daniella and the children returned with their stack of twigs and branches. He had found an ax in the plane and used it to chop several of the tree branches that had become impaled in the plane into small, manageable pieces. They had enough wood to last them for at least a couple of days.

Since they were in the middle of spring, Richard was thankful that at least they wouldn't have to worry about snow or freezing temperatures. Several of the extra emergency blankets were used to create a tentlike area. The blankets resisted tearing and did not shred like other blankets. Upon further inspection, Richard wasn't pleased when he discovered that the plane lacked some other critical emergency supplies, forcing them to be creative.

James Baxter positioned several of the magnifying lenses up in the trunk of several trees nearby. Water was an essential survival item that would be in great demand. Wendell surprised everyone by his ability to locate a small brook nearby, that was down in a small crevice hidden by several large boulders. While the survival cooler had a water supply, he and Richard knew that it would probably not last more than a day or two, and they had no idea how long they would be stranded.

Glenda also proved useful, volunteering to make dinner by creating a somewhat unappetizing combination for their evening meal, but everyone was too hungry to make any complaints.

That night as the group settled in to sleep, Stephen, the slimmer Baxter brother, tried to keep the mood up.

"It's like we're part of *Gilligan's Island*," he said.

"Gilligan who?" Mrs. Pruit said.

"Not who, what."

"Gilligan's Island," his brother said.

"What about it?"

"He was comparing our predicament to that show," Daniella said. "It was a TV show about strangers who are stranded on an island."

"After their plane crashes?"

"No, it was a boat."

Mrs. Pruit shook her head. "Then I don't see how it applies to us."

"Don't you watch TV?"

"Not that kind."

"I've never seen it," Anna said.

"That's because you're too young."

"You can see reruns," Daniella said.

Richard sent Daniella a curious, teasing glance. "So should I call you Ginger or Mary Ann?"

She couldn't help a smile. "I preferred *I Dream of Jeannie,*" Daniella said, referring to the classic '60s sitcom about a genie and her astronaut-master.

He nodded. "Me, too." A grin tugged on his mouth, lighting his eyes. "Go on and say it."

She blinked, feigning innocence. "What?"

"Yes, Master."

"You're not an astronaut."

He leaned toward her, the fun light in his eyes becoming a warm glow that drew her in. "I could take you to the moon in other ways," he said in a husky tone.

She bet he could and she'd enjoy the ride. "Now

who's dreaming?" she said, meeting his steady gaze, wanting to run and stay at the same time.

"I think I'll call you Ginger. Glenda can be Mary Ann."

"And are you Gilligan?"

He shook his head. "No. The professor."

The next day Daniella ignored him. She did her chores, glad that everyone did their part, but kept as much distance from him as she could.

"You stupid girl!" Mrs. Pruit said.

"What is it?"

"She spilled my drink."

"I didn't see it. I just accidentally—" Glenda already sounded as if she'd given up, knowing Mrs. Pruit wouldn't listen.

"I bet you did it on purpose. Since the crash didn't kill me you'd like me to die of thirst and to fade away from dehydration."

"That's not true."

"So that you can have my son all to yourself."

Daniella took her cup and poured some of her water into it. "You can have some of mine."

"Thank you."

After averting that disaster Daniella went to check on Herman, who had barely eaten last night and hadn't eaten much that morning. When she saw Richard she called him over.

"I'm worried about Herman. He's unusually quiet."

"He's fine." Richard continued what he was doing.

"He's not fine."

"Leave him to me."

"You're covering for him."

Richard didn't reply. Instead he walked over to the copilot.

"What did he do," Daniella continued. "Fall asleep?"

Richard spun around so quickly she knew she'd uncovered the truth. Her eyes widened as everything came together. The pilot had had a heart attack and when the plane nosedived the sleeping copilot must have fallen forward and hit his head.

Richard returned to her and kept his voice low. "Don't say a thing."

"But that's criminal."

"What's criminal was the schedule he was given." Richard shook his head before Daniella could speak. "Look, he's got a family to support."

"And I'm supposed to care? What if you hadn't been on the plane? We'd all be dead."

"But we're not."

"Fine, I won't say anything, but I bet you the others will have their own questions."

"We'll handle them."

Daniella folded her arms. "I'm sure you will. Is there a pilot honor code or something?"

Richard took her hand and led her over to Herman. "Give me your wallet," he said to him. When he did, Richard opened it then handed it to Daniella.

She saw a color photograph showing three smiling children. "I get it, he has a family."

"More than that, he could lose everything."

"He'd probably just get suspended."

"You don't know what it's like to lose everything you love. To have everything you care about on the line."

"I'd never take the risk."

He snapped the wallet closed. "Sometimes you don't have a choice."

The man who called himself Richard Engleright knew Daniella was a distraction for all the wrong reasons. He'd already forced himself to get over the fact that she was one of the most beautiful women he's ever seen—and in his travels he'd seen a lot. No, it wasn't that. Or even that her lush, curvaceous figure—he'd imagined her naked twice—at times had him mesmerized. It wasn't even the fact that she managed somehow to look both sexy and sweet. No, it was her strength that pulled him to her the most.

She had a quiet energy that made his life easy, by allaying fears and calming tension. She was able to keep everyone's spirits up. He barely slept the next night. He couldn't afford to because not only was she strong, she was smart. He knew she wanted to know more about the crash and about him, especially where or how he'd learned to fly but he wasn't going to tell her. He didn't want to explain his background, but he was thankful that his training had come in handy, especially since he hadn't used it in years. He'd been able to steer the plane from an inevitable crash that would have killed all aboard. When he felt the plane plummeting and the pilot hadn't been able to pull up quickly, he instinctively knew something was wrong. Very wrong. And he was right. When he entered the cockpit he found the pilot dead, the copilot *not* sitting in his assigned seat, unconscious probably from hitting his head when they lost altitude. Richard knew the copilot must have been dozing or something, but there was no time for him to waste trying to assess what had happened, he had needed to land the plane safely.

Fortunately, they had been flying over a very dense area, and he was able to successfully maneuver the plane close to a column of tall trees, using their tips to help absorb and slow the plane enough for him to make a safe, although bumpy, landing. He'd gotten them out safely, but now he found himself in danger from a curly haired woman with a bright smile. Here he was supposed to think of survival and at every turn she was there or in his thoughts. She tempted him without trying—especially her mouth. Every time she opened it he wanted to dive inside. He could imagine doing a lot of things with that mouth and having that mouth reciprocate in kind. Her lips would be wet, warm and sweet. Yes, he would bet it was sweet. He groaned at the thought. He had to get over it—get over her and the feelings she stirred up in him. He was a man of control and he'd use it now.

On the third day the copilot had a slight relapse and suffered a seizure. This clearly indicated to Richard that his injuries were more extensive or serious than he had first identified. One of the children, the boy, kept having hysterical crying fits that woke him from his dreams all through the night, keeping everyone awake, because he was convinced that they were all going to die. Mrs. Pruit's demands had become more oppressive; then they had to deal with Glenda's mental instability, which was beginning to unravel. She had walked off that evening into the bushes without telling anyone. When she didn't return, the Baxter brothers had to go and find her. Daniella tried her best to stay upbeat and positive, but she too had begun to have doubts. Why hadn't they been found yet? Was anyone looking for them? What would they do if they ran out of food? At one point she looked at Richard, watching him secure the stakes that held up the makeshift tent. She knew he could read the fear in her eyes.

"It's going to be okay. Trust me," he said in a gentle tone.

But at that moment Daniella wasn't so sure. Who was this man that she should put all her trust in him? What if he decided to run off and save himself and leave them to survive on their own? He was willing to cover up for the copilot, a man he did not know. He had nothing to lose and since he was in excellent physical shape he would probably be the one to survive, along with the slimmer Baxter brother. The women would never make it, or the children. Glenda and Wendell already looked pale and were showing signs of dehydration.

No, stop it, Daniella thought. She had to pull herself together. Richard was all they had. She had to trust him. Even though she had doubts, it was clearly evident that the children didn't. They stayed close to Richard and he seemed to calm any fears. Anna and Mark followed him wherever he went and Richard never lost his temper with his new sidekicks. They slept near him, ate near him and talked to him. Daniella guessed that they were desperate for a father figure and he filled the role.

On the fourth day Daniella felt Richard watching her as she did her chores. Her first task was to help the children bathe in the creek Wendell had found on the first day of their ordeal, giving Richard a needed break from them, although he hadn't complained. A short distance away she watched Richard remove his shirt and she had to admit that her imagination hadn't done him justice. He offered a spectacular view. He was beautifully made but he was also strong and potentially lethal. She was glad he was on their side. She noticed a tattoo with the words The Sheppard Saints. Daniella wondered what it meant and what the significance was for Richard. He certainly wasn't a saint by any stretch of the imagination. More like a fallen angel.

"I'm not trying to start a coup," she said to him later in the evening. They had eaten the last meal of the day and Mark and Anna had fallen asleep, giving him some freedom. The others had also gone to bed and they both found themselves together. Alone.

"What?"

"And I'm not going to say anything about Herman."

He narrowed his eyes. "What are you talking about?"

"The reason you keep watching me."

He sighed, scratching the stubble on his cheek. The facial hair made him look even more The Renegade— just sexier. "Oh, that."

"Yes, that."

Richard ran a hand down his face. "I can't help myself." He winked. "I like the view," he said, his gaze dipping to her trousers and top, sliding over every curve of her figure as if he were slowly undressing her.

Daniella folded her arms, feeling her body grow warm. Did The Renegade just wink at her? "You like watching me?"

His gaze remained lowered, rising up to her chest then resting there. "No."

She lifted his chin. "Look at me."

His voice deepened with appreciation. "Trust me, I am."

She shivered and felt her heart lurch in anticipation, of what, she wasn't quite sure. But the air around them suddenly felt electrified. "I want you to look at my face."

His eyes met hers. "This better?"

Much. She licked her lips, gripping her arms tighter to herself. The entire world seemed to fall away, all her fears and worries disappearing with it. All she thought of was him and how safe she felt with him. "What do you want?" she asked, her voice barely a whisper.

"Do I need to spell it out for you, Ginger?"

"No, Professor." Daniella took a small step backward.

"What were you doing on this flight anyway?"

"Visiting my lover."

Richard shook his head. "You don't have a lover. You probably have a nice steady boyfriend who treats you like fine wine and tells you how beautiful and wonderful you are."

Daniella was annoyed by how close to the truth he was. She had, but she didn't anymore. "I do have a lover."

"Does he mind sharing?"

Daniella's heart began to race. "What?"

He curled a strand of her hair around his finger, his

knuckles brushing against her cheek. "How come I always have to repeat myself with you?" he said, his breath warm against her neck.

"Because you say outrageous things."

"Is it so outrageous that I find you attractive?"

"You don't even like me."

"You and I both know that's not true. I like you very much." His gaze trailed the length of her. "Remember you're Ginger not Mary Ann, stop being naive."

Daniella folded her arms, suppressing a grin. In truth she wasn't naive at all, but usually men didn't notice. She knew that the tight pair of trousers and red rayon top, from the limited selection in her suitcase, flattered her figure in more ways than one. Her travels around the world as a writer had provided her with ample opportunity to expand her horizons. She'd experienced fun, danger (usually no more than getting lost in a strange city), and romance. She had lots of opportunity for romance from Italian men to Kenyan men. She didn't sleep with them; she didn't have to. They adored her anyway. They were flattered by her attention and the fact she noticed that they existed. She'd learned the delicate and effective art of stroking a man's ego early. She loved men of all colors and creeds, but knew better than to let them get past her facade of naïveté, afraid she might scare them off. However, Richard was something else entirely. He challenged her, teased her and didn't seem afraid at all. She had to be careful of him. "Did you find some liquor on the plane?"

"You think a sober man wouldn't find you attractive? That's a pity."

"No, I just think you're acting strange." She never doubted her beauty, why would she?

"The fact that we're still alive makes me believe in miracles." Richard held up Daniella's hand, in the cool evening air his hand felt exceedingly warm. "Is your lover the one who gave you this?" he said, staring at the antique ring she wore.

"No, my sister Izzy gave it to me along with a pair of matching earrings. It was an extravagant present, but she wanted me to have it when I sold my first major story."

He frowned. "You're a reporter?"

"No," she said, knowing she should draw her hand away, but also knowing she wouldn't. "I'm a travel writer and I do freelance work." She glanced down at the ring. "The only reason I always wear it is because it's like carrying my sisters with me wherever I go. Twice I've been offered a lot of money to sell it and the earrings, but I never will."

Richard lifted Daniella's hand and kissed the back of it. The touch of his lips on her skin made her mouth go dry and she wished that he'd kissed her lips instead of her hand. "I don't blame you. It looks good on you."

She drew her hand away and gripped it into a fist, annoyed with herself. She had to remember that he wasn't for her. Too dangerous. "There's another young woman you can focus your attention on."

"She's married."

"After spending these days with her mother-in-law she may change her mind. You could persuade her."

"I'd prefer to persuade you."

"Why?"

"Because you've been sweet to everyone else and I want you to be sweet to me."

Daniella was slightly taken aback by how bold and direct he was. "How?"

He moved closer. "Kiss me."

"Is that an order?" she teased, stalling to make sure she was ready to take the leap that was before her.

"I could make it one. But I hope I don't have to."

Daniella recognized the challenge more because of his intense, smoldering gaze than by his tone—although she had to admit that was just as inviting. She leaned forward, ready to fulfill his demand on her terms. "All right," she said then touched his lips with hers, wanting to give him a quick, indifferent kiss, but he didn't give her the chance. The moment their lips touched a rush of emotions assailed her body and his arms circled her waist and brought her close. He pulled back a moment and stared at her in wonder. "It's amazing."

"What?" she breathed, equally in awe.

"You actually taste as sweet as you look." He kissed her again before she could reply. His hand snaked up her shirt, cupped her breasts. "How come I don't scare you?"

"Who says you don't scare me?" Her heart was beating fast from pleasure, not fear, and she was breathing so shallow she was afraid she'd either faint or he'd kiss her to death.

"You wouldn't be touching me like this if I did."

She glanced down at her hands and saw she'd removed the buttons to his shirt. "I shouldn't be doing this."

"Yes, you should. Keep going."

"We hardly know each other."

"My name is Richard," he said then captured her mouth again. It was so warm and inviting that it took her away from all her fears. No, he didn't frighten her but maybe he should.

She quickly pulled away. "No, I'm not doing this."

"You want this as much as I do," he said in a low velvet tone. "Do you need a reason to continue? I can give you a few." He caressed her cheek and again she marveled at the strength and tenderness she felt in his hand; that a man of such power could be so gentle amazed her. "I risked my life for you, and you want to give me a reward."

"Wouldn't you want something more substantial?"

He cupped her breast again. "You're substantial enough."

She pushed his hand away. "That's not what I mean."

"Come on. Admit it."

"What?"

"You like me." He held up his hand before she could argue. "Yes, you do. Okay, you need another excuse so we can continue? I also cleaned and bandaged your wound. You can thank me for that."

"I already thanked you."

"You can thank me again." Again he gave her no opportunity to refuse him—not that she would have— capturing her mouth in a hot kiss that made her think of warm, dark nights, tumbled sheets and melted candles.

Richard pulled away, a smile of triumph crossing his face, hinting at a vulnerability she hadn't expected to see. She sensed not only triumph but relief as if he hadn't been sure of her feelings. It seemed strange for a man who seemed to be sure of everything. "I'm glad you're not afraid of me."

A sharp cry interrupted Daniella's reply.

"Richard!" Anna cried out.

He didn't move, still gazing at Daniella as if in a dream. "Richard!"

Daniella tugged on his sleeve. "I think you should go."

His face fell. "What?"

"Anna's calling for you."

He sprang into action and raced over to the child. "It's okay. I'm here." He pulled her onto his lap and cradled her with a back and forth rocking motion.

Anna sniffed. "I woke up and you weren't there. I thought you'd left us."

"I just went for a walk. I would never leave you. Now go back to sleep."

"Are you going to sleep, too?"

"Yes, in a minute." He quickly calmed her down.

"Is she going to be okay?" Daniella asked, coming up behind him.

"Yes. I guess we'll have to call it a night."

"Why did you hesitate?"

"What?"

"When she first called you, you didn't respond." She laughed. "It was as if Richard wasn't your name."

"I was too busy enjoying you."

"You don't look like a Richard. The name Richard

doesn't suit you," Daniella said, adjusting her still partially unbuttoned shirt.

Richard stiffened. "What kind of name do you think would suit me?"

"I don't know. I'd have to think about it."

"Don't think too hard."

"Don't worry. Once I lie down and close my eyes you'll be out of my mind."

He gave her a featherlike kiss that felt like a breeze slipping through the trees. "No, I won't," he said then got up, turned and walked away. He climbed into his survival blanket and went to sleep, leaving Daniella's lips warm and wanting.

On the fifth day they finally heard the sound of a helicopter. Richard and the men sprang into action. Stephen ran out into a clearing in the field and started setting off flares. Wendell and James climbed two of the nearby trees and retrieved the reflecting mirrors and joined Stephen adjusting them manually to get the sun's rays, hoping to catch the pilot's attention. The two children were wildly running in circles and jumping up and down calling out to get the pilot's attention. The helicopter circled once then went away and within a few minutes returned, flying low. One of the rescuers onboard put their hand out the window with a thumbs-up, indicating they saw them. They were rescued at last. While Mrs. Pruit insisted that she had to be the first person airlifted out, the copilot and the two children were the ones who were selected to be transported first. The helicopter had to make a total of three trips before everyone was safely out. Because of the terrain and location where the plane had landed, it would have taken hours for a vehicle to reach them and days for rescuers to arrive on foot.

The copilot was taken by Medivac to a hospital at least forty-five minutes from the location where the plane had crashed. The other passengers were all taken to a nearby local community hospital where they were examined and all deemed to be in good health, except for Mrs. Pruit. Due to the fact she had not been taking her diabetic and blood-pressure medications—she had refused to bring an extra supply—she was extremely dehydrated and had to be admitted for several days to bring her pressure and blood-sugar levels down, both of which were at dangerously high levels. Unfortunately Glenda had to endure those days in the hospital, alone, without any support. Thankfully, her husband, Thadius Pruit, would be joining her in two days. For the entire five days the plane had been missing, he had been trying to get back home. He had been traveling in northern Nigeria and, unfortunately for him, Nigerian airline workers went on a massive work strike and he found himself stranded. He had to take a total of three planes and travel by way of Nigeria to Egypt, London to Seattle, then Seattle to Kennedy airport in New York.

Daniella, the Baxter brothers, Wendell, and Anna and Mark were all put on separate flights and sent on their way. Oddly, Richard disappeared as soon as they landed and Daniella didn't get a chance to thank him for being their hero. The whole rescue scene had been so climactic. Upon arriving at the hospital they had been surrounded by the press and bombarded by reporters, each one eager to get a firsthand account of the accident and how they, the passengers, had survived.

"Where did you find water?"

"What about food?"

"What happened to the pilot? Do you think he was negligent?" On and on, the questions would not stop.

While Daniella had obliged and granted a few interviews, she kept most of the story for herself. She knew a story about surviving a plane crash would make for great journalism.

Once home, Daniella decided that she wanted nothing to do with The Renegade. He hadn't even taken the time to say goodbye, which explained why she hadn't thought of him as a potential story, but now she did. She thought of all the different angles she could come from in order to make her story engaging. She desperately wanted to show Pascal that she was as serious a writer as he was and not just some travel writer.

The doorbell rang.

"Oh, that would be for you," Sophia said.

Daniella frowned. "Why for me? I'm not expecting anyone."

"You are now. I called your sisters."

Chapter 3

"Why?"

Sophia flashed a sheepish grin. "I thought if I couldn't convince you not to go off on your crazy scheme maybe they could."

The doorbell rang again, this time insistent.

Daniella covered her eyes and groaned. "Tell me you didn't call Mariella."

Sophia jumped up and ran toward the kitchen. "I'll get us something to drink."

Daniella swore and stood as the bell rang a third, fourth then fifth time, each time more demanding. "I'm coming!"

She swung the door open and saw her two older sisters. One with a welcoming grin the other with her arms folded: Isabella and Mariella.

Mariella's eyes flashed. "You really shouldn't keep

people waiting." She entered without waiting for an invitation.

"She didn't know we were coming," Isabella said.

Her sisters were opposites in both temperament and appearance. Mariella, the eldest of the four Duvall sisters, was a tall, striking beauty with skin like polished oak. She had traveled the world as a model and later as a renowned photographer. Isabella, the second eldest, was petite with ordinary features but had keen dark eyes and a warm smile.

"We need to talk to you," Mariella said, walking past Daniella in a haughty manner.

Daniella sighed. "There's nothing to talk about. Sophia made a mistake."

"She doesn't make mistakes," Mariella said, entering their small living room and taking a seat on the couch. She held out her jacket for her younger sister to take care of. Daniella put it over the back of an armchair behind her against the wall.

"Just bear with us," Isabella said in a low voice as she gave Daniella a quick hug.

"I can't believe Sophia called Mariella," she whispered back.

"She cares about you."

"Calling Mariella for advice is like using an ax to cut a cake."

"What are you two whispering about?" Mariella said in an impatient tone. "Come on. We don't have all day. This isn't a family reunion."

"No," Daniella said. "Those are supposed to be pleasant occasions."

"Are you saying you don't want us here?"

Isabella held up her hands. "Let's just get this over with. Dani we came because—"

"We want to stop you from making a huge mistake," Mariella finished. She crossed her long legs at the ankle. "Sophia told us that you want to go after a man."

"That's not what I said," Sophia said, entering with a large tray of lemonade, juice glasses and cookies.

Mariella dismissed her objection with a quick wave of her perfectly manicured hand. "Well, that's what you meant."

"No, I—"

"We think that's a dangerous idea," Mariella cut in, leaving Sophia with her mouth open.

"I'm not going after a man," Daniella said with a tired sigh. "I'm going after a story."

"Same thing."

"You have plenty of stories," Isabella said. "You don't have to chase after this one." Daniella usually listened attentively to her older sister. Any advice she gave seemed to always be tempered with a certain amount of wisdom. But this time was different. She didn't need advice, she'd already made up her mind.

Daniella leaned forward, eager to get her friend and sisters to understand. "I want the challenge. I think I can get him to talk to me."

"Ginger?" Sophia said.

Daniella paused, remembering the name Richard had given her. But how could she have known? "What did you call me?"

Sophia frowned. "I didn't call you anything. I was referring to the cookies. Do you want ginger or cream?"

Daniella shook her head, feeling her heart return back to normal. "I'm fine."

"The last time I spoke to you," Isabella said while pouring everyone a glass, "it sounded like you already have enough assignments and you usually get the 'go-ahead' from different editors. How are you going to afford this little venture of yours?"

"I plan to use some of my savings and presently, my schedule over the next couple of months is clear. Besides, since I work freelance, I can schedule my own time."

"What if you dedicate all this time and no one wants the story?" Isabella said. As part of her responsibility for being the second eldest, Isabella seemed to spend most of her time worrying about her two younger sisters. She knew Mariella would and could take care of herself.

"Besides," Mariella added. "Didn't you already write a piece about the accident and get it published? Or is this some other story? I'm confused."

Daniella gripped her hands together. "It won't be the same story."

"But who will be really interested anymore? It's been almost five months since the accident happened. All the notoriety has already died down."

"They'll want it," Daniella said, determined.

The doorbell rang again.

Daniella turned to Sophia, amazed. "You called Gabby, too?"

Her friend shrugged and stood. "I wanted to cover all bases," she said then opened the door.

"Sorry I'm late," Gabby said. She was the third Duvall sister and had Isabella's kind smile and Mariella's good looks, although she was the most full figured of the four sisters. "Did I miss anything?"

"We're just getting started," Isabella said.

Mariella held up her hand. "I've said all I need to."

Gabby hung up her coat in the hallway closet, greeted her younger sister and then took a seat beside Isabella. "I don't blame you for wanting this man, Dani, he sounds amazing and so mysterious. I only saw a grainy image of him when the story was printed in the newspaper article you sent us about the accident. And I liked what I saw."

"I don't want *him,*" Daniella said, losing patience. "I just want *his story.*"

"What does he look like?" Mariella asked.

Gabby looked at her sister, surprised. "You haven't seen him yet?"

"I've been busy," Mariella replied, helping herself to another ginger cookie.

"The only man she notices is Ian," Isabella teased, referring to Mariella's new husband.

"The pictures I've seen haven't been that good anyway," Gabby said, trying to be fair. "He really doesn't like the camera and keeps his head lowered. You can only see his profile."

"I bet you, that just getting a good shot of him would be a coup," Sophia said as she keyed something into her cell phone.

"You're not helping," Mariella said with a frown.

"Just a comment."

"Here's a picture," Sophia said holding up her phone for everyone to see.

"Hmm," Mariella said, leaning in to get a better view.

"He's delicious," Gabby said.

"Why is everything a food reference with you?"

"I like food." She bit into one of the six cookies she'd taken.

Mariella gazed over her sister's full figure. "No one would argue that."

"Mariella," Isabella scolded.

Gabby raised her chin. "I don't care, Tony likes me just the way I am."

Sophia waved her phone before Mariella could respond. "Do you want to see him or not?"

Mariella squinted at the image. "You can hardly see anything."

"I'm using my imagination," Gabby said.

"He could certainly rescue me," Isabella added.

"He's not that good-looking," Daniella said.

"Yes, you're right," Mariella agreed. "He has a hooded look. I've never liked that in a man. And his mouth is too grim, his jaw too prominent and harsh and his skin—"

"He's not that bad-looking," Daniella said defensively.

"I didn't say he was bad-looking," Mariella said then began to smile.

Daniella inwardly groaned realizing she'd been tricked. She shook her head then folded her arms. "It's not like that. I just want this particular story. I've always been interested in investigative journalism and now I have a perfect opportunity."

"And when did that start? When you were traveling to all the finest restaurants in Paris? Or when you were mountain climbing in Japan?" Mariella said.

"Don't make fun," Isabella said. "She's serious."

"Only because Pascal dared her to do it," Sophia said.

Mariella checked her manicure. "I don't believe in challenges like that. I find them childish." Her three sisters looked at her dumbfounded, remembering the time several years ago, when the four of them had made a pact to snag a certain man who was a promising catch for one of them.

"It isn't a dare," Daniella countered. "It's a chance to expand my portfolio." And to prove that she was a serious writer. Editors only gave or accepted simple fluff pieces from her. She wanted more: more exposure, more pay, more respect. "I've made up my mind. Please let me live my life. I've never told any of you what to do and you've all done crazy things."

"Like what?"

"Go after a man just for his money."

"That's not fair," Mariella said. "You tried to, too."

"Yes, but Gabby ran off with her fiancé's best friend. And you smuggled drugs for the man you loved!"

"I did not! It was all a misunderstanding!"

"And what about Ian?"

Mariella tensed. "What about him?"

"There are still rumors that he married his father's mistress."

Mariella jumped to her feet. "How dare you! You know that's not true. I never—"

"Then don't read things into my life, either."

"I'm leaving. Where's my coat?" she began pacing, but going nowhere.

"Sit down, Mariella," Gabby said.

Mariella grabbed her jacket off the chair and headed for the door.

"Coward," Isabella said in a quiet voice.

Her sister spun around. "What did you say?" She took several steps toward the group.

Isabella stared at her unfazed, used to her sister's outbursts. "You're being stupid. Now sit down."

Mariella rested her hands on her hips. "Why is everyone picking on me?"

Isabella patted the empty seat beside her. "Daniella has a point. We can't tell her how to live her life when we've made interesting choices of our own."

Mariella returned to the couch with a scowl that did nothing to mar her pretty features. "You're just trying to be so-called fair, because she hasn't said anything about you."

Isabella turned to Daniella with a curious expression on her face. "No, she hasn't. What do you want her to say about me?"

Daniella couldn't stop a smile. "Nothing. There isn't anything to say."

Mariella rolled her eyes. "That's only because her life is boring."

"That's not true," Gabby said. "She ended up marrying my ex-fiancé. I don't think that's boring."

"Only because you practically left him standing at the altar. She was a consolation prize."

Isabella playfully slapped her sister on the arm. "Oh, thanks a lot."

Mariella grimaced. "I didn't mean it like that."

Sophia rested a hand on her chest signaling her loyalty to her sister-in-law. "I, for one, know that my brother is very happy with his choice and so am I."

Isabella grinned. "Thank you."

Mariella held up her hand. "We've completely veered off topic." She pointed at Daniella. "You don't have to listen to me or any of us, but I just feel that you're going to get into some serious trouble if you have anything to do with this man."

"First of all he's too old for her anyway," Sophia said.

"I don't want him!" Daniella said exasperated. "I just want to write a story. I'll be safe. You don't need to worry about me. I've traveled the globe more than four times alone and I've always returned home safely."

They ignored her.

"He's not that much older," Isabella said. "And besides, Gabby married an older man."

"Older men are well seasoned, and can teach you quite a few things," Gabby said with a sly grin.

"You can teach the young ones, too," Isabella said with a sly grin of her own.

"What about a man who has been married before?" Sophia said. "He's probably set in his ways."

"You can still change certain traits or ways that irritate or annoy you," Mariella said with confidence.

Daniella jumped to her feet exasperated. "Stop it!

Just stop it. You're all missing the point. I don't want him as a man. I don't need a new relationship right now. Richard Engleright is my ticket to a new life. A promotion where I will command admiration, where people come to me for advice, where editors clamor to give me assignments and accept whatever I send them because they know it will be good and they trust me. That's all. I've been traveling and writing about fantastic places around the world, and I have done well for myself. But I'm ready for a change. I'm ready to try something different."

"We're not here to stop you," Isabella said.

"Yes, we are," Mariella countered. "You're on the rebound from a terrible relationship with a bore. I don't know why you still have anything to do with Pascal."

"He's brilliant."

"Maybe, but his manners are why you dumped him. And nobody likes Pascal except you and I think it's cruel that he'd taunt you so much that you feel you have to go after this stranger, who has the right to be left alone."

Daniella shook her head. "I just—"

"I haven't finished. What you're prepared to do is to go after a complete stranger whose past could be hidden for a reason—a dangerous one. I'm older. I know that life has a dark side—every person, too. If you dig deep enough you may find something you're not prepared for and can't handle."

"I don't care."

"That's the problem," Isabella said. "You should care. This is a big undertaking and we just want you to weigh all of the risks."

I have and it's worth it, Daniella thought, but knew it was best to keep her thoughts to herself. "I will."

Mariella stood. "Good. Now that that's done I'll see you later."

Gabby left with Mariella, and Sophia disappeared into the kitchen. Isabella looked at Daniella for a long moment. "Did he kiss you?"

Daniella stiffened. "What?"

Isabella raised her brows. "You heard me."

"Why would you ask me that?"

"So I guess that's a yes."

"I didn't say yes."

"You don't have to. I was curious at first because of how determined you were to convince us that you only saw Richard as a story instead of a man." She grinned. "Now I don't have to be curious anymore."

Daniella didn't want to talk about kissing him, stunned by how quickly she could remember the feel of his lips on hers and the touch of his hand as it skimmed across her skin.

Isabella's grin grew. "Ah, yes, that's what I thought. He's more than just a story."

"That's not why I'm going after him."

"Whatever your reasons, be careful." She sighed. "No matter what I say you still want to find out more about him, don't you?"

Daniella knew she could lie, but Isabella would see right through her. She nodded.

"Then go for it."

"To be honest, I don't even know where to start."

Isabella paused then said, "Was there anything about him that really stood out?"

Daniella thought for a moment then snapped her fingers. "His tattoo."

"That's a good place to start. I've heard that tattoo artists have signature looks. Someone could give you a lead, just be careful. I'm not trying to scare you, but you know how Mariella's hunches have a way of coming true so be careful. If you ever need anything you know we're here for you." Her sister rose and gave Daniella a big hug.

"Thanks, but this is something I have to do on my own."

Daniella drew a quick sketch of Richard's tattoo from memory then posted the image online asking if the image looked familiar to anyone. Over the next seven days she received many replies. Most of them useless. One respondent thought that the tattoo was a rip-off of a comic book hero; another thought that the wearer was part of a secret alien race. After weeks with no decent leads, Daniella was about to give up when one email caught her attention. She opened it:

I know that tattoo. I believe it belongs to my missing son. Why do you want to know about it? Please call me at…

His missing son? If he was his son, why would Richard be missing? It couldn't be the same person. Maybe a group of guys got together and got the same tattoo.

"Call him," Sophia urged after Daniella showed her the message.

Daniella paced. "It just seems wrong. How could Richard be missing?"

"You won't know until you find out. Look, if you want to back out now I understand."

"I don't want to."

"Then why are you stalling? You've gotten this far, why stop now? Whether it's this guy's son or not you have to find out the truth."

"I know."

"You've already raised this poor man's hopes. There's no turning back now."

It was a definite lead. She licked her lips then dialed the number.

"Hello?" a deep voice answered. It was gravelly but warm.

"Yes," Daniella said in too high a voice. She cleared her throat and tried again. "Hi, this is DD," she said. She'd decided not to list her full name in the email, only her initials. "You responded to my post about the image. You said you think that the tattoo belongs to your son."

"Yes, my wife wasn't too sure of my answering your email because there are a lot of crazies on the internet. But something about your query seemed genuine and I trust my instincts."

"Yes. And you think it belongs to your son?"

"I know it does. Only four of us have that particular tattoo. I have it, so does my son and two others. The words stand for a group we were all part of when my son was younger. Also, his tattoo has a unique extra marking, which I recognized in the sketch you posted. Why are you looking for him?"

"He saved my life and I wanted to thank him, but he disappeared before I had a chance." At least that wasn't a complete lie.

"That sounds like my son. He doesn't like to take credit. How did he do it?"

"Do it?" Daniella echoed, confused.

"Save your life."

"Oh. We were on a small plane that was about to crash and he—" She heard the man catch his breath. She stopped. "Sir?"

"I thought that might have been him," he said amazed. "I read the story in *The New York Times* about the crash and the passengers surviving in the forest for four days, but I wasn't sure. Marnie! This girl has found Trenton!" he shouted to someone who was there with him.

Trenton? "No, wait, there may be a mistake," Daniella said quickly. "The man I'm looking for is called Richard Engleright."

"I don't care what he calls himself now. I think that you could be our chance to get our son back."

Daniella hesitated. She would hate to raise their hopes and then dash them. "I think I should do a bit more background and research first."

"We can give you all the background you'll need. Could you come see us?"

Daniella paused. "Can you hold on a minute?" She put the phone on hold and sat. She looked at Sophia. There was no turning back. She had to do this. She reconnected. "Okay, let's meet." She got the information she needed and agreed to a meeting. When Daniella hung up she remained silent. Sophia shook her. "Well?"

"I'm going to Pennsylvania."

Chapter 4

This has to be a mistake, Daniella thought as she drove up the gravel driveway leading to the expansive house ahead. Somehow she'd expected a small, stately home, but this one was moneyed. No, this couldn't be the right people. She felt her heart sink. She could call and cancel. She could tell them that she didn't think it was the right fit and just leave. She started her ignition, then saw a short, stout woman rush out of the house.

The woman came up to the car window and tapped on it. "Daniella?"

Daniella suppressed a groan and shut off the car. She couldn't escape now. She got out of the car and plastered on a grin. "Yes. I wasn't sure I had the right place."

"You do. You must be tired after such a long drive. I have refreshments waiting inside."

"Thank you." The woman looked so hopeful, but she

also looked nothing like Richard. She had bright, beaming brown eyes and a face like that of a young girl's although she was clearly a woman in her sixties. She had an ageless glow. Maybe he took after his father.

"Come in," Mrs. Sheppard said. "My husband went to run an errand. He'll be back soon."

Daniella followed Mrs. Sheppard inside the house and the moment she did so she felt instantly at home. They lived in a split-level with a large picture window showing a view of an enormous back garden filled with an array of colorful flowers. The walls were painted a soft peach, with off-white trim that contrasted wonderfully with the polished oak floors. Mrs. Sheppard led her to the main living room, where Daniella settled into the large corner seating arrangement that almost filled the room. In the middle of the room, she spotted a teapot and cookies on a center table.

"I can't tell you how happy we are that you've found us," Mrs. Sheppard said while a dour-looking woman entered and took Daniella's handbag and coat.

Mrs. Sheppard rushed ahead and lifted the plate of cookies. "I've been hoping for this moment for years."

Years? Daniella took a bite of her cookie and chewed slowly, hoping to come up with a delicate response. "Mrs. Sheppard, I don't want you to—"

"I wasn't sure when Gilford told me about you, but after meeting you I'm sure. You were meant to come into our lives and help us find our son. I read your article about the crash. It was very powerful."

Not cute? She wished Pascal had been around to hear her. "Thank you, but I'm not sure yet that I—"

They heard the front door open and Mrs. Sheppard jumped to her feet as if on springs. "That will be Gilford. Excuse me."

Daniella glanced around the room, but didn't see any pictures of Richard or Trenton, or whatever his name was. Perhaps it was too painful? She buried her head in her hands. She would hate having to give them the bad news that she didn't really know their son. Especially when they seemed so certain. Daniella glanced up when she heard footsteps approaching and saw a figure disappear behind a wall. The housekeeper, maybe? Or just her imagination? She didn't get much time to speculate because Mr. Sheppard entered the room displaying a big smile. He looked like he could pass for a black Father Christmas. There was no resemblance to the hard man she'd met months ago. She looked at the couple and couldn't see Richard in either of them. How could such warm, loving people have such a hard, distant son?

Daniella stood and shook his hand. "Before we continue I think we should stop speculating."

"You're not sure he's our son?" Mr. Sheppard guessed.

"You're both such such lovely people." *And unless he was adopted I think we're talking about two different men.*

He reached into his back pocket and took out a photo from his wallet and handed it to her. "Is this the man you're looking for?"

Daniella took the image and saw a good-looking man smiling. He stood in front of a plane, holding a puppy in his arms while a gorgeous woman in a sleek dress, with a short pixie haircut and three-inch high heels, stood by his side. Her heart sank. "No, this isn't—" She stopped when she focused on his mouth—that was familiar. She looked closer to make sure. Yes, his mouth and those lips she remembered, her gaze drifted up to his eyes, but they were nothing like what she remembered. The brown eyes in the picture were bright, hopeful and happy. It couldn't be him…but then again she remembered his eyes after he'd kissed her and how they seemed to glow, transforming his face. This picture of him looked like it was taken a lifetime ago. She slowly sank into the chair. It was him. But what had happened to him?

Mrs. Sheppard stood beside her. "Is it him?"

"Yes," Daniella said. "But he doesn't look like this anymore."

"We know," Mr. Sheppard said with a weary sigh.

"After the accident and divorce he was never the same," Mr. Sheppard explained.

Daniella frowned, remembering Richard—Trenton talking about an old injury. "Accident?"

Mr. Sheppard nodded, seeming to age years, the weight of his loss a constant companion. "Look up Trenton Sheppard on the internet and you'll find all you need to."

"Except the truth," Mrs. Sheppard said.

"Yes, except that."

"He won't talk to us. We'll get a postcard every year, but that's it."

"Last one had this postal code." She handed Daniella the card. "We hired a private detective but nothing has worked. You're our last hope."

Daniella gripped the postcard. *No pressure there.* "I'll see what I can do."

"I know you will, but I want you to know more about him first. I hope you don't mind but it's been so long since we've been able to talk about him like this and we feel the more you know the more you'll understand him."

I doubt it. "Sure."

Mrs. Sheppard pulled out an album and opened it. "This is Trenton with his sister and their first pet, Bobo. He was devoted to that dog and when Bobo got arthritis in his hips Trenton made him a wheelchair of sorts. He always loved to help…" She went on to tell Daniella about his Boy Scouts days, his days at school, how popular he was and how marrying Fayola had been the happiest day of his life. She then got to the accident. "He said something was wrong with the plane, but no one was able to prove anything. I know my son wasn't negligent and didn't cause the crash, even though he was blamed for it."

Mrs. Sheppard wiped away tears. Her husband gently patted her on her back. "It's going to be okay, Marnie. We'll get him back."

"When you see him—" Mrs. Sheppard began.

"You mean *if*," Daniella corrected.

"No, I mean *when*," she said with certainty. "Because I know you'll find him and when you do, please tell him to 'keep the flag flying.'"

Bonita Zarro watched the stranger drive away then picked up the phone. "A woman came by asking about him."

"Who?"

"You know. The Sheppard boy!"

"So what?"

"What does she want with him? Why is she asking questions?"

"Who knows? Who cares? It has nothing to do with us."

"You don't know that."

"Have you been drinking again?"

"I haven't had a drop in years and you know it. I think we should tell Dr. Brooks."

"I think you're blowing things out of proportion."

"I don't."

"Fine, I'll tell him. What's her name?"

"Daniella Duvall and I think she's one to watch."

"She can't do anything and neither can Sheppard. He knows what's at stake."

"Sometimes a person needs a little reminding."

Bonita set down the phone.

"Who were you talking to?"

She spun around and stared into the hard glare of her boss, Mr. Sheppard. He seemed jovial and nice when he wanted to be, but she knew he had a cold, ruthless side. He was smart and she had to be careful.

"Nothing. I know I'm not supposed to make personal calls on duty."

"Are you sick?"

"Why?"

"I noticed on my ID that three calls have been made to a Dr. Brooks and I overheard you mention his name."

She'd been careless. In her panic she hadn't thought that it would matter.

"Yes, I had an appointment, but I canceled."

"Okay." He walked away.

Dr. Brooks had made sure that she got her current job with the Sheppards. She couldn't afford to lose it. Not with her record. And they were good people who treated her well and she didn't want to have to leave them.

She would be careful. No, she had to be.

Daniella drove home feeling as if she could fly. She had a real name now and a lead. She was gaining on her target.

At home, she didn't bother to change her clothes or get something to eat, but went directly to her laptop, went online and looked up Richard's story. What she read made her heart break. Trenton Sheppard used to be a medic pilot. He was on an emergency rescue flight, when they encountered really bad weather. He was forced to make an emergency landing, and although there was plenty of space for him to land, he had somehow veered the plane off to the side and it had gone into a lake nearby. The pilot, medic and nurse all escaped, but although they tried to rescue her, the patient they had been transporting, a young woman in her early thirties, could not be extracted from the plane in time. She drowned.

In the days and weeks following the accident, an investigation resulted in Trenton being indicted for negligent manslaughter based on the fact that drugs were found in his system. Although he had denied the drug accusation, the lab results provided undisputable evidence that he was under the influence. He was stripped of his pilot license and fired from his job. While he did not face any jail time, his career was ruined. He was also sued by the victim's family. He lost everything. His house, cars, boat, savings, investments and his marriage.

Daniella sat back remembering his words: *You don't know what it's like to lose everything.* This had to be what he was talking about. But a drug addict? He didn't seem the type, and besides, his parents believed him. But they seemed the type who'd believe in the tooth fairy. Daniella knew she needed to remain skeptical. She needed the hard journalist edge that Pascal thought she lacked, and yet…she believed them, too. Richard—Trenton seemed too disciplined and focused to be the type to lie about what really happened. Then again, he could be good at keeping his addiction hidden. She knew of a prominent actor who had been an addict for years, but was a high-functioning addict who had no trouble getting and keeping great movie roles. But then again, you can never really know anyone. For a moment Daniella felt conflicted, but soon switched her thoughts to her memory of the middle-aged couple she had just met. Perhaps, if she could find him she could convince him to return home. His parents obviously missed him. She decided she would write a reunion story. The prodigal son returns home.

Daniella closed her laptop. No, she had to focus on the hard story. His past. She could just hear Pascal telling her she'd written another cute story. No more cute stories for her. She was determined to get to the truth.

She drafted an outline for the article then sat back, satisfied, and called Pascal, ready to hear him eat his words.

"I found him," she said when Pascal picked up.

"What?"

"Richard Engleright. I found him."

"How?" Pascal said, clearly stunned.

"I remembered his tattoo. I just came back from meeting his parents."

"And you'll talk to him next?"

"Yes, but I have to still do more background investigating because this guy has quite a story. First, his real name isn't Richard, it's Trenton and I already have the angle I'm going to use. I'm sending you my draft."

"I can't wait to read it."

"Impressed?"

"Very," Pascal said with a laugh. "I'll never call your work cute again."

Chapter 5

Vera Clegg had lived in Sykesville, Maryland, all her life. She'd buried her parents, sister, husband and a still-born daughter there. She was used to the town's strange ways and its people. She looked over at her daughter Emma and sighed. She had to do something about her. Emma was getting up in years and her looks had never been a strong point and were already quickly fading. She had skin like sun-bleached wicker and limp black hair that barely reached her shoulders. She was a good girl, kind, generous of heart, but shy and clumsy. Vera cringed as she watched Emma knock over a salt shaker and apologize to a customer.

In the background was the sound of sizzling bacon, while cutlery scraped across dishes amongst a cacophony of conversations. The breakfast crowd had gone, but they were still busy. If her brother didn't own the diner where they worked, she'd likely have been fired years ago. But she, like the diners, was a fixture, and people liked to see her, which helped to offset her daughter's less than stellar qualities.

Vera looked around the diner and let her gaze settle on booth twelve where a woman Vera didn't recognize finished her breakfast. She was definitely an outsider. Her clothes didn't say "city," but she certainly wasn't "mountain." Her movements were too refined for that. She buttered her toast as if she was using fine silverware, and she looked like the type of woman who wouldn't know the difference between a tractor and a riding lawn mower. She didn't belong there. But Vera could guess why she was there—she was a reporter. A whole bunch of her type had come into town, bugging poor Richard, when all he wanted was to be left alone. Fortunately, they learned fast that they couldn't push him around and they couldn't find out anything from the townsfolk either. They soon lost interest and vanished. This woman would do the same if she had anything to do with it.

She approached the table. "How's your food?"

"Lovely, thanks."

Lovely? Perhaps she was city after all. "What brings you into town?"

"Just passing through."

"You're looking for Richard, aren't you?" She began to smile at the look of surprise on the young woman's face. "How do I know? Because we rarely get newcomers, especially young ones. So are you a reporter?"

"No."

"Ex-wife?"

"No."

"Girlfriend?"

"No. He saved my life."

Vera lifted a sly brow. "And you're here to thank him?"

To her surprise the young woman didn't look embarrassed or flustered, she just held a calm, steady gaze, which made it hard to tell exactly what she was thinking. "How long have you lived here?"

"All my life," Vera said, surprised by the question. But she wouldn't be distracted. "You might as well turn back right now."

"Excuse me?"

"You're not going to get whatever you've come out here for. You're too soft to ask hard questions, too weak to get past his guard and too young to know your limitations. You're not his type, honey. So if you want to thank him, just send a card."

The woman smiled, unfazed. "I thought only customers were supposed to give tips."

"It's not a tip. Just some plain old-fashioned advice."

The woman stood. "Thank you for your advice."

"You're not going to listen to me are you?"

She paid her bill.

"You're going to get your feelings hurt," Vera said as she watched the woman walk out the door.

"Eight thousand dollars?" Trenton stared at his vet, Dr. Khan, a straightlaced man with a bushy mustache. "But I don't have eight thousand dollars."

"She needs the surgery."

"I know, you've made that clear but…" Trenton let out a tired sigh. After losing his job and getting his divorce he'd barely managed to stay afloat this long.

"She's really sick and the tumor is growing fast," Dr. Khan continued. "The medicine keeps the pain to a manageable level but it only hides the symptoms."

"How long does she have?"

"Three months, maybe four."

Trenton hung his head.

"There's another option."

Trenton looked up hopefully.

"You could put her down."

"No."

"I'm just laying out your options."

Trenton shook his head, adamant. "No, I'll figure out something."

"Do you have any kind of pet insurance?"

"Hell, *I* don't even have insurance." He stood and held out his hand. "Thanks for what you've done."

"I haven't done anything yet."

"Thanks anyway. At least I know what I'm facing."

Moments later, Trenton helped Layla, his beloved golden lab, into the truck. It was getting harder and harder for her to make the leap from the cab of the truck to the driveway. He sat beside her and stared out the windshield. She nudged his hand and he petted her then she licked him, making him smile. "You don't even know that you're dying, do you?"

She licked him again.

"Or maybe you do and you have just accepted it."

But he couldn't. Layla was all he had left. She'd been his companion for seven years: through the scandal, his eventual dismissal and the disintegration of his marriage. Without her there would be nothing left. *Eight thousand dollars.* Money he didn't have, but he'd have to find a way to get it. He turned on the ignition. Unfortunately, he had nothing of value to sell. He'd sold everything so that he could live a town-to-town existence, which is what now made up his life. It was rootless, and consisted of him not settling or staying in one place for too long. Hell, he couldn't even sell his story about the recent plane crash and how they'd survived in the wilderness, although reporters had been eager to write about him. He was likely old news anyway. Besides, he couldn't risk public scrutiny even with a fake name. Somehow his past would be uncovered and then all that interest would turn to shame and disgust. Besides, he knew that it would only reveal that he was no hero. Something he'd once wanted to be.

As a child he'd devoured comic books and video games. On the playground he had been the rescuer. Off the playground he would save neighborhood pets like his best friend's rabbit when it got swept down a drainpipe, or find a cat when it had gotten lost. His father, a doctor, let him pretend to bandage him up, giving him gentle correction when he made it too tight or too loose. His life had been privileged—graduating from college with honors, his parents were proud. They were even more proud when he married.

Everything was perfect until the accident and the fallout. He knew his parents wanted to believe in his innocence, but he still couldn't look his father in the eye, just in case he saw a hint of doubt. That would crush him. They had been there with him throughout the entire trial and afterward. He had been reduced to moving into their house after his wife left him and he was basically penniless. His parents had paid all his court expenses, but he didn't want to live off them for the rest of his life. So, following the verdict and then the civil suit that was brought a couple months later, his only choice was to get out of town. He hadn't meant to hurt them, and wished he could see them again. He missed his mother's home cooking. She was originally from the Bahamas and loved to cook his favorite treats. He missed spending time with his father, who was a Southern boy who knew how to cook anything on a grill. Remembering those times filled him with a deep ache. At times when he closed his eyes he could picture zucchini on the grill, hear his mother humming as she baked. Most times though, what he missed most was flying. He remembered taking his father on his first solo flight, and seeing his father's face beaming with pride.

But that didn't matter now. They still had his sister and her family to dote on. Their disgraced son would never darken their world or cause them any more anguish. They were better off without him. Everyone was. Where he lived now, way up in the mountains in northern Maryland, seemed so far from his years growing up in Delaware and Pennsylvania. The rush of excitement of his old life was far removed from the quiet small town he now called home. He felt bad taking off for good. His original plan was to escape for a few days.

He needed to figure out how to rebuild his life, but as the days passed he came to realize that there was nothing to rebuild. He could never live again, he'd always just exist. That's what he deserved. He had dedicated his life to helping others but had ended up taking one instead. Now he worked as a volunteer emergency medical technician, or EMT as they were called, with the local fire department and made extra money doing odd jobs, and that was fine with him.

When Trenton reached his property, he drove up his long driveway and spotted a car. He hit his steering wheel and swore—it was Vera's. He'd been warned about her, but hadn't listened. One day he'd made the mistake of offering her a smile and accepting her offer of a free cup of coffee and a doughnut. He hadn't been able to get rid of her since. An attractive woman of fifty-three, she treated him like a son, which meant she thought all his business was hers, too, and she rarely gave him space. What was worse was that she kept trying to fix him up with her daughter, Emma.

He thought of backing out but she saw him and waved. He faked a quick grin and waved back. He groaned when he saw her open her trunk; that meant she planned to stay awhile.

"Layla, if you want to run away, I understand," Trenton said in low tones as he got out of the truck. He noticed Vera was carrying a basket of food and resigned himself to his fate. At least that was something she and her daughter knew how to do and he was a man who enjoyed a good meal.

"Well?" she said as he walked up to his house.

"Well what?"

"I know you took Layla to the vet. What did he say?"

Of course she'd know, there were few secrets in Sykesville, except his past. Trenton went up the steps and put the key in the front door lock and turned the handle a bit too hard as he remembered the outcome of his visit to the vet. "He said I need eight thousand for surgery." He looked at Layla, who had decided to stop and rest beside the truck. The late-spring sun touched her golden coat making it seem to sparkle like an angel. No, he wouldn't think about death.

"I'm sorry."

"Hmm." He went inside knowing he didn't need to offer Vera an invitation, she would come in anyway, which she did and pushed past him to head into the kitchen.

Trenton set his keys on the counter. "I told you that you don't have to cook for me."

"Someone has to look after you." She opened his fridge. There were three bottles of beer, a carton of juice and a half-eaten loaf of bread. "I rest my case."

"I eat in town," he said, watching her put several packs of herbal teas in his cupboard. Emma was always giving him tea, even though he was a solid coffee man.

"Rarely. You're too skinny. You need a woman."

"I had a woman."

"You need another one."

Trenton hesitated, wanting to choose his words carefully. "Vera, Emma is a very nice girl. I'm just not looking for that right now."

"Nothing's wrong with being friends."

"We are friends."

"You could be close friends."

"I'm not close to anyone."

"Still, you haven't invited her over for a while."

"I've been busy."

"You work too hard." She finished stocking his fridge and closed the door. "Oh, by the way, there was a woman looking for you."

Trenton paused. "A woman? Looking for me?"

"Yes, asking questions."

"Oh, another reporter," Trenton said, losing interest.

Vera shook her head. "Nope, not a reporter. She didn't give off that energy. She's not aggressive enough. Very composed, but definitely not hard-edged."

Could Fayola have found him? Damn, after all these years did she still think they could get back together? Had she changed her mind and realized she'd been wrong about him? Why did he still care? He had no one to share his deepest pain—that of losing his wife. They had met while he was at university. He was a senior, she was a freshman. He waited three years before they got married. He remembered knowing she was his soul mate. Her father was Nigerian and her mother was from the South, similar to the cultural mix of his family. They both took pride in their heritage and firmly enjoyed spending time together watching their favorite sports teams from home. She loved cricket while he loved soccer. They both loved to dance and couldn't find enough time going to different restaurants and dancing venues for all-night dates out. She was all that he had wanted in a woman. Smart, confident, beautiful and sexy. They had so many plans for the future; a home in Nigeria and a vacation home in South Carolina. They would have three, no two children, a boy and a girl... Richard snapped out of his fantasy... No, it couldn't be Fayola. She had no use for him now, but maybe... "What did she look like?"

"Like a sugar plum fairy."

He frowned. "What?"

"You know," Vera said with an impatient flick of the wrist. "All sweetness and light, like a gingerbread cookie. She had a mess of curly dark blackish-brown hair, big brown eyes and cupid bow lips."

No, that definitely wasn't Fayola. No one would ever describe her as sweet. Sweet would describe that woman he'd met after surviving the crash. The one with cheeks like caramel apples, hair like cotton candy and lips like strawberries dipped in melted sugar. But she was more than just sweetness, she had an iron will. She'd taken control after he'd landed the plane and he'd depended on her to follow his lead. If he'd had a chance he would have led her down a more passionate road than that of a simple kiss.

"So you do know her?" Vera said, sending him a curious glance.

"Who?"

"The woman I just described. The one at the diner."

"No, I don't." He blinked. "Why would you say that?"

"Because you're smiling. You don't do that often."

Trenton let his smile fall. "I was just remembering something." No, it couldn't be her either, but it was a nice thought. "I really have some work to do."

"Well, I just thought I'd warn you. She seems determined to talk to you."

"Don't worry, Vera. I'll handle her. Whoever she is."

Duane Martin slammed down the phone and sat back. The bastard was still alive. Dr. Brooks had called him, saying some woman was searching for Sheppard and knew where he was. He'd always known that it was possible that Sheppard was still alive, but had somehow hoped it wasn't. "Time heals all wounds," his therapist had said, but he knew that was a bunch of crap. Years later and the death of his wife still tore him up. He'd spent a year in Japan and another in Turkey just to get rid of every memory of his old life. It hadn't worked. He'd meditated, fasted, juiced, cleansed but nothing seemed to work. He even tried a brief affair, but it just got messy. He felt himself slowly growing crazy.

He picked up the newspaper Dr. Brooks had sent him and gripped it when he saw the grainy image. He saw the face of the man who'd stolen his life from him. Who'd forced him to bury his hopes and dreams for the future. They were calling him a hero! He sank down into a chair and read the story again, trying to keep the bile from rising in his throat. No, maybe he was just a look-alike. They were calling this guy Richard Engleright.

But no, he'd recognize that bastard anywhere, no matter how much time had passed. Dr. Brooks was right. The only way to get his life back was not to run away, but to confront his fears. He'd show the world who Richard Engleright really was and now he knew where to find him.

Chapter 6

She wasn't going to make it. Few cars made it up his front driveway. He'd designed it that way, so he always took the back route to his house, which only a few town regulars knew about. The front entrance was an obstacle course that consisted of deep inclines, ruts and rocks. Trenton saw her car tire get stuck and grinned, pleased. Now he had her, whoever she was. She'd probably call a tow truck service to help. He started to turn when he saw the woman get out of the car. His heart stopped. *Damn, it was her!* He'd recognize that mass of hair anywhere. Even from this distance she had that calm, sweet quality he'd seen on the plane and after the crash. She was a great person to have at one's side at a time of tragedy—a man could use a woman like that. He didn't even have to imagine what she felt like or how she tasted because he knew. He'd been glad to take the chance when he could. She'd given him some nice memories. He knew that she'd not only be great by a man's side, but in his bed, as well. He frowned, annoyed by his thoughts. Some other man. Not him. Still, he watched her, mesmerized, as she seemed to assess the situation then glance around. She spotted a board and placed it under the tire. He felt a smile on his lips. Smart girl. She was resourceful, he had to give her that. She got in the car and drove over the board and up the drive only to face another obstacle—a fence with a bolt lock no one could get past. Sorry, Ginger, you're not welcome on this island.

Drat. Daniella pounded her steering wheel. She hadn't expected this. Why would there be a fence in the middle of a driveway? It wasn't as if it was a working farm or a ranch, from what she could see. What was he keeping out or in? She instinctively knew that the only way to get past was to leave her car and either climb over the fence or go through it. She was small enough to go through it so she left her car and lifted one leg between the bars and began to shimmy through.

"What do you think you're doing?"

Daniella froze then looked up and saw The Renegade. His name still suited him. His eyes were still hard. His jaw harsh. The sun behind him seemed to make him appear larger than she'd remembered, then she recalled the picture his mother had shown her with his first pet Bobo, and giving his sister a piggyback ride. Soon, she also noticed how the sunlight softened the rough angles of his face. She remembered the concern in his voice when she'd been hurt, his tender touch, the soft feel of his lips. No matter how ferocious he tried to be she didn't fear him. She flashed a shy smile. "I'm coming to see you."

"Why?" There was no welcome in his voice.

"I have a few questions."

"You drove all the way out here to ask me a few questions?"

"Just give me a minute…" She shimmed through the wooden slats, falling on the other side of the fence with a thud. She looked up but Trenton didn't offer her a hand. She sighed and stood, dusting herself off. He was a hero, not a gentleman. The fact that anyone thought she had designs on him as a love interest amazed her. No accounting for taste. He was not relationship material. He was good for a brief love affair and nothing more—he had heartbreaker written all over him. Besides, no matter how good a lover he was she didn't need that right now. She had to focus on her career and proving Pascal wrong. She couldn't—wouldn't—be distracted again. Trenton was only a great story, that's all.

He rested against the fence. "What's your question?"

"Questions," she emphasized. "And why don't we go inside and—" She stopped when he shook his head.

A grin tugged at the corner of his mouth. It wasn't a friendly expression. "That's not going to happen."

"What?"

"I'm not letting you inside my house so that you can snoop around and try to uncover dirt about my life."

"I'm not a reporter."

"But you are a writer. I saw your notes on the plane."

"Yes, but—"

"I don't have anything to say to you or anyone."

"And I understand that but—"

He pushed himself from the fence and gestured to her car. "Good, then I'll see you on your way."

"Let me just…" She paused then shoved him to the side and ran.

Trenton watched, stunned, as she darted past him. Was she a crazy woman? He hadn't noticed this strange behavior when they were together during the four days they had been stranded. She was probably good at hiding her mental issues. Maybe she'd try to tie herself to his porch until he answered her questions or break into his house. He ran after her then immediately saw why she had taken off. Layla was having a seizure. Daniella fell on her knees and immediately touched the dog gently, smoothing its fur and tenderly soothing the animal until the shaking subsided.

He watched in amazement as she lifted Layla up and stumbled back under the weight of the animal. Trenton hid a smile. "Give her to me."

"I'm fine. Open the door."

He did. Daniella started to follow, but he blocked the entrance. "I said I'm not letting you in my house and I mean it." He took Layla from her.

"But what's wrong with her?"

Her concern was real and he felt it more than he wanted to. "Goodbye, Ginger," he said then kicked the door shut with his foot.

It was a few moments before he heard her footsteps leave and then he watched her drive away. He was a little sorry to see her go. She had been a nuisance but had broken up his usually boring day and taken his mind off of what his real trouble was. He looked down at Layla, who had quickly recovered from her episode. "She's not coming back so don't look so hopeful. I know you like her, but you like almost anyone." He patted Layla on the head, remembering Daniella's tender touch and the true concern he'd heard in her voice. She was just a busybody, nothing else, and those kisses in the woods were just that—nothing. Over. In the past. Even though when he licked his lips he could still remember the taste of her and how good she'd felt against him. He shook his head. He had enough complications in his life at present; he didn't need to invite trouble.

"I'm glad she's gone," he said to Layla wondering if he was trying to convince himself or if he meant it. It was stupid hero worship that would take its course and disappear. What would happen when all that was stripped away and she was just left with the man? He was glad that she hadn't said anything about the copilot and they'd come up with a credible story that had kept the reporters happy and allowed Herman to keep his job. At least for the first time in a long time he'd been part of a happy ending. He'd stopped believing in them.

Daniella remembered the sight of the closed door as she finished her lunch at the diner, which consisted of a grilled salmon burger and chips. Her first attempt hadn't gone well, but she wouldn't give up.

"Told you it wouldn't work," Vera said as Daniella

drank her grape juice. "I can tell by your face that you didn't get anywhere with him."

Daniella merely smiled.

Vera took a seat inside the booth. "Why don't you leave the poor man alone?"

Daniella calmly sipped her drink. Women like Vera didn't frighten her. With a sister like Mariella all women paled in comparison.

A woman in a diner uniform came over and said, "Uncle Lincoln has a question for you."

Vera sighed then looked at Daniella. "Do the right thing and just forget about him," she said then left.

"Sorry about her," the other woman said removing Daniella's empty plate. Her badge had the name Emma, although the name didn't seem to suit her. Perhaps because of the book by the same name Emma implied grace, sophistication and elegance. This Emma showed no sign of those features. She was plain-faced, but had good bone structure she hadn't highlighted. She clattered the cutlery and dishes together which grated on Daniella's ears, but she seemed friendly so Daniella didn't mind. "That's okay. I understand people looking out for each other."

"No, Mom is just nosy."

Vera was her mother? Daniella felt sorry for her, but knew that she could be useful. Vera may want her gone, but Emma seemed friendlier and more open. Daniella offered her a reassuring smile. "I don't mind. My mother passed away."

"I'm sorry. You can have mine if you want. She thinks of herself as the mother of everyone sometimes.

Richard's been through a lot and we like to look out for him."

"That's admirable. What do you know about him?"

"That he likes to keep to himself. None of us really know what he's about or much about him. He just showed up one day."

"No wife or kids?"

"Not that we know of."

"What about you?"

"What about me?"

"Have you and he ever gone out?" She doubted it, but asked anyway.

Emma colored and shook her head. "Me and Richard? No...no...never. We're just friends. If you knew him you'd know I wasn't his type."

"He doesn't seem to be the kind of man to have a particular type."

"He does. Mom saw a picture of a woman in his house once, very stylish. But he's packed it away because she hasn't seen it since."

"Obviously he'd gotten over that. A man's type can change."

Emma shook her head again. "I'm not interested anyway."

Daniella wasn't sure she believed her. Emma looked ripe for romance and likely craved the attention of men. Why she would set her hopes on Richard, Daniella could only guess. He wasn't the romantic type. Although he did have his moments. She thought of him teasing her about her lover, calling her Ginger. Yes, he had another side, but still remained guarded. Emma had likely been very sheltered and didn't know she had other choices.

"Sure, I understand. But you do like men, right?"

"Yes." Emma ducked her head like an embarrassed ostrich. "But they rarely notice me."

Daniella could see why. She wasn't much older than Emma, but looked decades so. "It's because you don't give them anything to notice."

Vera's voice cut through the diner chatter. "Emma, stop yakking and get back to work."

The young woman turned, looking guilty. "In a minute, Mom." She looked at Daniella with hope in her eyes. "What did you say?"

"Nothing really," she said with regret. She didn't want to hurt Emma's feelings, but she seemed eager to talk and share. She was a woman in need of a friend. "I hope you don't take this the wrong way."

"I know I'm not fashionable."

Not even close. "You have a nice face that you hide and your clothes…" She let her words die away as a thought came to her. Perhaps if she did Emma a favor she could help her with Richard. "I've just had an idea. When do you get off work?"

"Um…eight."

"Emma!" Vera said.

"Okay." Daniella quickly took out a card and scribbled down her room number. "Come by the bed-and-breakfast after you're done and we'll talk."

"About what?"

"Your makeover."

Emma's eyes widened. "You'd give me a makeover? But you don't even know me."

Vera's voice grew louder. "Emma!"

"You'd better go before you get in trouble."

"I'm always in trouble with her. I'm her big disappointment."

Vera came up to the table. "Emma, when I call you I expect you to answer."

"It's my fault," Daniella said without apology. "I didn't mean to keep her, but we were having a fascinating conversation."

Vera looked unconvinced. "Sure you were," she said but she didn't argue as she pushed her daughter ahead of herself, nudging her forward to clear another table.

That night Daniella sat in her room and waited, not sure that Emma would have the boldness to come. She glanced at her watch. It read 9:15 p.m. Fine, Emma likely wouldn't show. Even if she couldn't give her any information about Trenton, she would have liked to help her. She really seemed in need of a friend and needed a new look desperately. Before going back to her room at the bed-and-breakfast, Daniella had gone to the local drug store to pick up some cosmetic supplies. She'd give them to her anyway. Emma was too old to be that bullied by her mother. Daniella was flipping through the four channels the room offered when there was a light knock on the door.

Daniella answered and Emma rushed in. "Sorry I'm late."

"That's okay. I'm glad you came." The girl looked like a wilted weed. She reminded Daniella a little of her older sister Isabella before she fell in love with her husband, Alex. "Let's get started."

"I don't know much about makeup. Mother says my coloring's all wrong."

"Your coloring is just fine."

Daniella immediately went to work. Having a sister as a fashion model had given her a great advantage. She knew how to use minimal makeup to totally complement, not mask, a person's face, and how to emphasize anyone's best features. Emma's eyes and mouth were definitely made for color. Her eyes, while they appeared dull, were a beautiful toffee color with yellow highlights. Putting dark purple liner on both her lower and upper lids gave them an sultry look. She used a small amount of dark brown foundation to emphasize and outline her cheekbones, which combined well with her rustic medium-brown skin color.

Next she applied lipstick, resulting in a pair of delicious, kissable lips. Daniella used a basic foundation that matched Emma's skin tone perfectly. The entire procedure took less than fifteen minutes. Her hair, however, proved to be somewhat of a problem. It was limp and unconditioned and was in desperate need of a cut. Daniella decided against washing Emma's hair, especially since it was getting rather late in the evening. Instead, she grabbed a pair of shears and removed all the split ends. She applied a leave-in conditioner and a light moisturizer that added sheen and volume. Then she took her handy shears and began trimming away until she had taken Emma's shoulder length hair and given her a layered medium-length style. The result was stunning.

"You know there's another way to reach Richard's house," Emma said. Daniella had mentioned the earlier incident of getting stuck in Richard's driveway while she painted Emma's nails a bright purple. Emma's choice, not Daniella's.

"There is?"

"Yes, the back way. When we're done I'll give you directions."

"Thanks. I'd appreciate it." Daniella finished the manicure then took Emma into the bathroom to look at herself in a full-length mirror. "Now what do you think?"

Emma stared in amazement. "It doesn't even look like me."

"But it is you. You have excellent skin. I only added a little color to your cheeks and eyes. That's something you can do. I'm going to wipe this all off and I'll show you how to do this. It doesn't take long."

"Really?"

"Yes." She winked. "I bet the men will start looking now."

"How did you learn how to do this?"

"I have three sisters. Believe me, I had plenty of practice. And one of my sisters was a professional model."

"You've lived such a glamorous life."

Daniella laughed. "Not quite."

"I bet it's better than mine."

"You want to leave?"

"Sometimes. But then there's my mom. I'm all she has and I wouldn't want to leave her alone. Do you know what I'd really love?"

"What?"

"To become a grief counselor. I also study the healing effects of teas and give them to customers sometimes if I think they need it. I've lost so many people in my life and I like helping others. I think I know how to do it."

"Then start."

She ducked her head. "But I don't have the education or…"

"You can volunteer. You could start a small group with a few people or offer to listen to individuals one-on-one and provide them with an opportunity to share their feelings with you. Think about it."

"You make anything sound possible."

"Because it is."

"I believe you."

Once Emma was gone, Daniella planned her strategy for the next day. Anything was possible, which meant she could get close to Trenton if she tried hard enough. She didn't know why he was so adamant about being left alone and why had he isolated himself from his wonderful parents. She still didn't see them in him. He didn't have his father's build or his mother's eyes, but she couldn't deny the pictures. Wow, how things had changed from the picture taken of that young man standing in front of the plane to the man now living in the mountains. Daniella knew she'd have to play hardball if she wanted to get what she wanted. And she was ready to play.

Bonita Zarro had grown tired of living a lie. Her life had never been easy. She didn't know who her real parents were and as a child had been bounced from relative to relative until she ran away at fourteen. Thankfully, instead of ending up on the streets and having to sell her body, Bonita ended up in a youth program for underage runaways. She always thought a place called "home" was only a myth. People couldn't be trusted, they would only hurt you. She stayed away from drugs, but developed a drinking habit at age twenty that got her a few DUIs and a couple nights in jail. Bonita fell in love with a man who was no good and ended up having a son who was no better. By forty she was barely scraping by until one night after a party and a heavy night of drinking, she was walking in the middle of a street and got hit by a car. She sobered up that night and while she lay in the hospital bed she made a deal with God that if He let her live she'd turn her life around.

Bonita survived until morning and started to attend AA meetings. She left her sixth lover and became a janitor cleaning Dr. Brooks's medical practice. She liked the job, but regretted mentioning to her son that medicines were kept in the office. She should have known he would have seen it as an opportunity for no good. When Dr. Brooks discovered who had broken into his office, he didn't report the theft to the police or have her son charged. But it wasn't long before she realized there was a price to pay. She had to keep her mouth shut. Dr. Brooks helped her select a new name and identity. He created a new résumé and got her the position as a live-in housekeeper at the Sheppards' house. Bonita learned quickly what her primary duty was. At first she didn't care, thinking only about the money Dr. Brooks was giving her and how little she had to do. Under his direction, she had to make sure that specific calls didn't go through, and that certain messages got erased. But as time went on Bonita began to care for the Sheppards and their son.

Last night she'd heard Mrs. Sheppard crying again. She'd cried that way before, too, when that Daniella girl had come to talk to them, but she'd sounded hopeful and Bonita regretted making the call to Brooks. She wanted to see their suffering end. She knew she had a no good lout of a son, but they didn't. Their Trenton was a good man. She thought men like him only existed in books, but he was the real thing. She had been sorry to see his marriage collapse and the legal trouble he'd endured. She knew he hadn't been a user. She'd grown up around junkies and could spot them anywhere from street corners to Wall Street. It was like a sixth sense to her and she knew Trenton Sheppard didn't have an addiction. Unfortunately, there was nothing she could do when the lab work came back positive, convicting him. Besides, no one knew of her involvement, and her ability to sense his innocence wouldn't have mattered.

But things were different now. The Sheppards believed in her. They had taught her what a family was. When she'd had to have a minor surgical procedure they'd visited her in the hospital every day and had even bought her a beautiful bouquet of flowers. No one had ever done that for her before. For the first time she knew what home and family was about. They'd never mistreated her or hurt her, but over the years she'd been hurting them. It hadn't been intentional at first, she just thought it was a dog-eat-dog world. But they'd shown her otherwise. Now, as she sat on the edge of her bed in the mother-in-law apartment, she thought about what she might lose. But she wanted to stop Mrs. Sheppard's tears and knew the sacrifice would be worth it.

Chapter 7

Trenton woke to the sound of Layla barking. He went downstairs and looked out the window and saw a familiar car coming up the driveway, but not in the front, the back. He swore. She was good. She'd obviously convinced someone to give her the new directions. That was quite a feat because the townspeople were usually wary of outsiders but he could imagine her using those big brown eyes and enticing smile to get past their defenses. He swore again then ordered Layla to stop barking. He glanced at his watch. It was too early for this crap, and he wasn't in the mood to deal with her so he wouldn't. "It doesn't matter. She'll discover I'm not home." He returned upstairs to his bed. He heard the doorbell ring and then a knock. He just pulled up the sheets, shut his eyes and soon it went silent.

Two hours later, Trenton got up, jumped in the shower

and got dressed, then went downstairs and made himself some coffee. Layla barked.

He gave her an affection pat. "I know I'm running late, but we'll go out in a minute."

She barked again. He gave her a stern look and she quieted. It was a beautiful morning. Trenton was glad it was the weekend. He would drive to his favorite scenic location and go for a walk with Layla. He poured his coffee then went out on his porch and leaned on the railing, inhaling the aromatic scent of fresh evergreens. Layla barked again. "Quiet, Layla. It's not like you to be impatient. We'll go walking in a minute." He took a sip of his coffee.

"It's a perfect day for a walk," a feminine voice said coming up behind him.

Trenton jumped, spilling coffee down the front of his shirt. He swore fiercely, making up words of his own.

Daniella rushed toward him. "Are you all right?"

He took a step back. "What are you doing here?"

"I hope it wasn't scalding hot," she said, looking at the stain on his shirt.

"You'd like that, wouldn't you?" He slammed his mug down on the side railing, tore off his shirt and threw it on the ground—angry at her and angry at himself for being happy to see her again. She was just as lovely and fresh as a spring morning and he could imagine spending the day with her, but he couldn't and he didn't want to. "What the hell are you doing here?"

"I didn't mean to frighten you."

"I wasn't frightened," he ground out.

"You jumped nearly a foot."

"Stop exaggerating. Why are you still here?"

"So you knew I was here?"

"I saw you drive up. I thought by ignoring you, you'd go away." He picked up his mug and headed for the door. "Let me try it again."

"Don't forget your shirt," she said, holding it out to him.

"Keep it."

"Wait, I just want to talk to you."

He opened the door. "Come on, Layla."

Layla glanced at Daniella with a longing glance then did as she was ordered.

"Fine, you don't have to talk to me, but I do have a message for you."

He walked inside.

"Keep the flag flying."

He shut the door.

Strike two. Daniella stared at the closed door then the soiled shirt in her hand and sighed. It was now time for plan C. Unfortunately, she'd have to come up with it first. She was about to turn when the door opened again.

"What did you just say?" Trenton demanded.

"I want to talk to you."

"No," he said with an impatient shake of his head. "After that. You said you had a message?"

"Yes. 'Keep the flag flying.'"

"Who told you to say that?"

"Your mother."

Trenton's gaze grew menacing, as did his voice. "You spoke to my mother?"

Daniella swallowed hard and nodded. She would stand her ground and not be intimidated. "And your father, too. They really miss you."

Trenton stepped onto the porch and closed the door behind him with controlled anger. "What game are you playing?"

"I'm not playing a game."

He grabbed her arm. "You saw their fine house and nice things and thought you could get some money from them, right? Like the psychic who told them I'd died. Or the investigator who told them I'd changed my name and moved to Cleveland. You saw simple, honest folks you could manipulate. How much money do you want?"

"I don't want any money and I only found them because I wanted to find you."

"How did you find them?"

She chewed her lower lip. "Your father found me."

"How?"

"I asked about your tattoo."

He froze. "You lured him."

"No, I just wanted to find you."

"How much do you want? You didn't strike me as the type, but I don't put anything past anyone, especially when it comes to motivation."

"Look, my first motivation was just to tell your story. You know, the man behind the hero type of thing, but then after I talked to your parents I sort of made a promise to them that I'd find you and make sure you were all right and give you the message."

"So just out of the kindness of your heart, you spend

time and money to track me down to give me my mother's message." He shook his head. "No one's that noble."

"I'm not being noble. I can help you, Trenton."

"Don't call me that."

"Why not? It's your name and it suits you better than Richard, even though Richard is a nice name. I just—"

"What do they look like?" he cut in.

"Well, they're black."

He frowned at her attempt at humor and tightened his grip. "You have one minute to convince me you spoke to my parents."

"I gave you the message and it obviously meant something to you."

"That's not enough. What did they look like specifically?"

"Well...your father is tall with a pepper-gray beard and suspenders and your mother is a stocky woman with curly gray hair. To be honest they looked more like Father Christmas and his wife, and their house like a gingerbread castle."

"And I bet you felt right at home," he grumbled, sizing her up in a swift glance. "You'd fit right in."

"Excuse me?" Daniella said, acutely aware of his grip on her arm. He held her with a casual strength. He didn't hurt her, but she knew she wasn't going anywhere.

"Forget it." Trenton released her as if she'd become too hot to the touch. He took a step back and folded his arms.

Daniella took a step forward, desperate to close the distance—both physical and psychological—that he was trying to put between them. She had to gain his trust. "When I first met them I thought there had been a mistake. How could such a lovely couple have ended up with a mean son like you?"

He nodded. "I've asked myself that many times."

"Why are you hurting them like this? They love you so much. At least send them a recent photo or letter."

"Do your parents know what you're up to?"

"Probably."

"And they approve?"

"I'll have to ask them, the next time I visit their graves."

He sighed and his voice softened. "I'm sorry."

"So you see why I'm jealous. You have yours and you won't even see them."

"It's better this way."

Daniella shook her head in frustration. "But you're all hurting. I can feel it and I—"

"You need to leave."

"Let me help you."

"Why?"

"I can get to the truth."

"What truth?"

"About the accident. I did some research and read all about what happened. The crash, the lawsuit…"

Trenton gave a low whistle. "You have been busy. Did you also find out what my grades were in elementary school?"

"I wish you'd stop trying to be funny."

"You don't know anything."

"I know that you were involved in a crash that killed

a woman and that you were charged with negligence because they found drugs in your system."

He turned to the door. "Good, you got the whole story."

Daniella grabbed his arm. She knew it was a useless attempt; her hand looked like a child's against his large form. If he wanted to leave, he could and she couldn't stop him, but she'd still try to get him to listen. "No, I don't think so. Your parents don't believe you are guilty and neither do I."

"Why not? My wife certainly did, as did all my friends and colleagues."

"They were wrong."

Trenton glanced down at her hand on his arm, a pointed look as powerful as a touch. "How do you know?"

Daniella yanked her hand away and rubbed her hands together wishing he didn't have such a visceral effect on her. "Because I know you."

He flashed a cruel smile. "You don't know anyone. Trust me, I've made that mistake before."

"So somebody betrayed you?"

"This conversation is over."

"I trust my instincts. You're not a man to do drugs."

"I bet you still believe in Santa Claus and the Easter Bunny."

Daniella gripped her hands together as though in prayer. "Please let me help you."

Trenton's face softened and he reached for her then withdrew his hand and grasped it into a fist. "You're sweet, but you don't know what's at stake. Go home. Thanks for the message."

"Trenton, please."

He looked at her for a long time, letting himself admit that he was more than happy to see her. He was relieved. She knew about his past and still believed in him and wanted to help. He tightened his fists, resisting the urge to touch her and make sure she was real. It all felt like a dream. This sweet, sexy woman had tracked him down and used his name as if he mattered, as if he was important. It had been so long since he'd been called by his given name with any kind of interest. She said his name without disgust or judgment and he liked the sound. He realized how much he'd grown tired of being alone. How good it felt to have someone believe in him again. It amazed him that she knew about his past and still wanted to help him. Could he trust her? He wanted to. That tender touch and care she'd shown Layla was something he wanted for himself. And he wouldn't limit her, she could touch him everywhere. He knew she'd be smooth and soft in all the right places. He could just imagine her wild hair spread out on a pillow, those big eyes filled with pleasure that he'd given her. "Where are you staying?"

She furrowed her brows. "You're changing the subject."

"I know."

"I'm staying at Country Time Bed-and-Breakfast."

He nodded. "Good. If you're in the mood to do anything besides talking, call me."

She blinked. "What?"

Her bright-eyed naïveté was the sweetest of all. "Fine. Let me make it clear."

He drew her close and covered her mouth with his, hungry to taste her again. She was as delicious as she had been the first time he'd kissed her. He had never kissed a woman who made him think of his mother's home cooking. She was soft like a freshly baked loaf of bread, smelled like the cinnamon rolls his mother loved to bake on the weekends and yet dangerous and satisfying as his many salacious thoughts he'd dreamed about engaging with her.

Daniella felt just as at home as her hands cascaded over his bare chest. Her fingers tingled at the touch of him. She didn't remember dropping his shirt and arching into him. She just savored the assault of his mouth on hers in a reckless possession.

"Just as sweet as I remembered," he murmured.

"You, too," she whispered.

"I'm sweet?" he said doubtfully.

"More than you know."

His eyes clung to hers, searching. "Do you understand me now?"

"I don't think I can ever understand you."

"Come on, Ginger." He pressed his lips against her neck. "I'm not that complicated."

She felt her body grow warm and her skin tingled from the contact. His intentions were very clear and so were her emotions. She fought to stay focused on her goal. "Why don't we do an exchange?"

He looped his arms around her and smiled, intrigued. "I'm listening."

Daniella paused again, amazed by how a smile changed his face. It was unguarded, young and care-free. She saw the man he used to be and the man she wanted him to be again. "Not that kind of exchange."

His gaze dropped to the front of her shirt. "I'm not interested in any other kind."

She lifted his chin. "Are you really that lonely?"

"Stop selling yourself short."

"I'm not—" She stopped when she saw his grin widen and her heart jolted at the sight of the gleam in his eyes—the distrust and hurt gone. And in an instant she realized her true purpose. She wasn't there just for a story or to reunite him with his parents. She wanted him to be redeemed. This man deserved to get his life back. This was the man she'd been searching for all her life: a man of honor. "Please let me help you."

Trenton's grin faltered. "I've just told you how you can help me."

"Let me help you in another way."

"I'm not interested in any other way."

"I could tell your parents where you are."

He drew away, his playful mood gone. "Go ahead and break their hearts. By the time they get here I'll be gone and you'll regret it. Don't lift their hopes up for no reason."

"I don't understand—"

"Exactly." He threw up his hands. "That we can agree on. You don't understand anything. You don't under-stand the damage you've done just by coming here. If you want to help me, you'll go back home and leave me and my family alone." He pulled her to him, captured her mouth in one knee-melting, velvet kiss that promised a lot more. "That offer is always open," he whispered, his breath hot against her lips. Then he went inside and closed the door.

Daniella kicked the door. The man was impossible. She turned and leaned against the door trying to get her heart rate back to normal. She did want him and sleeping with him would be amazing. She closed her eyes and slid to the ground, her legs no longer able to support her as she thought of one night with him. She could imagine how his body would feel against hers, his mouth exploring every part of her, and she could picture herself wrapped around him. Her body craved every inch of him, his kiss had made her hungry for more, but a night with him wouldn't be enough. It wouldn't change the fact that she'd failed. She'd failed to get his full story—at least his side of things. Yes, she did know more about him than most, but what should she do next? She'd emailed some more of her notes to Pascal and he'd again been impressed with the information she'd been able to gather. He told her he could help her. She'd gotten further than he'd ever thought she could. She'd proven herself, but she didn't care about that. In the end she'd struck out. She'd run out of options. Trenton didn't want her help. Mentioning his parents had gotten a reaction, but not the one she'd expected. Perhaps if she came up with something more substantial he'd know he could trust her. Obviously he'd been hurt and betrayed in the past. She didn't blame him for his reluctance, he didn't know her. She'd have to find another way to gain his trust.

Inside the house Trenton let out a long, deep breath as he watched her go. Good, this time he'd gotten rid of her, but he'd never forget her. Damn. For a moment she'd made him think of his life before the accident. He wanted to ask her if his mother looked well. He missed the sound of his father's voice and the scent of his mother's chamomile tea. Damn it. She shouldn't have gotten their hopes up. What had hurt more was she'd gotten his hopes up, too.

Chapter 8

"Did you get my notes?" Daniella asked Pascal that evening.

"Yes, great stuff."

"I've reached a dead end. He refuses to talk and I still need more."

"Talk to the people involved with the case. They'll give you a different perspective."

"That's a good idea."

"I know. And talk to his parents again and see what more they can tell you."

Daniella returned to the Sheppards' house a few days later. "He's safe," she told them. "He's living in a small mountain town and he looks healthy. I gave him your message."

"I knew you'd find him," Mrs. Sheppard said.

"He's still not ready to discuss anything. I offered

to help but he shut me down," she said, feeling beaten and sounding defeated.

"He won't see us?"

"He's wary." To say the least, Daniella felt like a failure. In this short time she'd come to care for the Sheppards and wanted to help them reunite with their son. She knew how important family was. She couldn't imagine not seeing one of her sisters for years.

Their faces fell.

"But I'm not giving up," Daniella said, trying to rally their hopes. "Tell me more about the trial."

"Everything was against Trenton. He complained that something mechanical was wrong with the plane, but when the mechanic checked he said that there was no evidence that anything had been wrong with it."

"There are a few things you should know. Recently our housekeeper told us about a man we'd trusted. Dr. Brooks. He'd hired her to spy on us."

"Why?"

"She doesn't know and her story seems a bit far-fetched."

"But she sounded earnest," Mrs. Sheppard said.

"Who's Dr. Brooks?" Daniella asked.

"He testified at the trial."

"Slandered you mean," Mr. Sheppard corrected.

"He did his job."

"To think I'd ever given him a recommendation."

"You knew him?" Daniella said.

"Most of his life. He was my protégé. I saw something in him that I'd wanted to nourish because as a young man he had been interested in medicine as much as I was. Also, he and Trenton had grown up together. They'd been friends."

"It's too awful to think that he had anything to do with what happened, he was like family."

"Yes, but as time passed I saw that he seemed more interested in money than in helping people."

"You couldn't tell that from his first practice?" Marnie sniffed.

Daniella frowned. "What do you mean?"

"Brooks's medical practice was in, let's just say, an unsavory part of town. Most of his patients were drug addicts, not that there's anything wrong with that, but it made things hard for him at the time. One time a patient broke into the office and stole drugs. There was an article written about it in the paper."

"And the prosecution used him?" Daniella said, surprised by their choice.

"Yes. They came up with a valid reason, but I don't remember it right now. I think you should find out why he hired our housekeeper, Bonita, to spy on us."

Daniella believed the housekeeper's claim was a little far-fetched but decided to follow up on it. She spoke to her, but couldn't get much more information. She didn't know exactly what Brooks was after, only that he liked to know what the Sheppards were up to.

"Please don't let him know I told you anything," she said when Daniella ended the interview.

"As I stated before I won't breathe a word."

"The Sheppards are so good to me and I can't believe that they haven't fired me. I can't prove anything, it's my word against his and he has a reputation that's much better than my own. But I hope that what I've said can help them and their son. I want to pay them back."

"You already have," Daniella said, heading to the door.

"Be careful," Bonita said, but she refused to say why she felt the need to offer the warning.

Daniella disregarded the threat as she thought up her next strategy. First, she read the article about the break-in at his office and then she tracked down the nurse who used to work for him, guessing she would be a good place to start. Daniella offered to pay for lunch. The woman reacted as if she'd offered her the crown jewels. Nona James came to the restaurant dressed to the hilt, but Daniella could tell by the scuffed shoes and slightly worn dress and jacket that she had either borrowed the outfit, or got the items she was wearing secondhand. "I'd always wanted to eat here," she said, looking around like an eager child on her first trip to the zoo.

"Order whatever you want," Daniella said, feeling generous. She soon regretted that when the nurse ordered the three most expensive items on the menu. Daniella hoped what the woman had to say would be worth the expense.

"Tell me about Dr. Brooks."

"He's a good doctor. The patients loved him although I thought he could have set up his practice in a better neighborhood, but he said he wanted to help those that others have overlooked."

"I read about the break-in."

"Yes, unfortunately that was a common occurrence in that area. I didn't blame him shutting down his practice after the case and working with different clientele. But it was really just one patient he was trying to get away from. He was an addict who had failed every rehab he'd tried."

"Why didn't you move with Dr. Brooks to his new practice?"

"I quit after the court case."

"Why?"

"I discovered that some evidence was suppressed. There were some inconsistencies with the lab results, both from Dr. Brooks and the independent lab he'd recommended, but that wasn't presented. They just stuck with the proof that the work had come back positive for drugs. I knew that I couldn't work with a man like that so I left. He acts like he cares and all of his patients love him, still do from what I've heard, but there was something about him I didn't like. I didn't speak up because I knew it wasn't my place. I know those corporate suits from Sheldon phoned him a few times, but they were witnesses for the prosecution."

"Sheldon?"

"Yes, the company that builds planes. Or used to. I think they got bought up or something. Companies are always either getting bought up or going bankrupt, right?"

Daniella only smiled, hoping Nona would get to the point.

She waved her comment aside with an impatient gesture. "Anyway, that's neither here nor there. The important thing was that they proved that nothing was wrong with their plane and there was no malfunction, just human error. They found an expert who confirmed their findings. The prosecution's case was strong anyway. I didn't feel my suspicions would make a difference one way or the other." She looked at Daniella's plate. "Are you going to finish that?" Daniella slid her plate across to Nona having lost her appetite anyway. From what Nona had shared she knew that this story would be bigger than she'd imagined.

After lunch, Daniella knew what her next step had to be. She had to go to the man who'd cost Trenton his job, Dr. Brooks. The man the prosecutors had depended on to win their case. Back home Daniella did a quick online search and discovered he wasn't a hard man to find. Unlike Trenton, he wasn't shy of the cameras and had no reason to be. He was attractive and eloquent and she knew that stroking his ego wouldn't be too difficult a task. She picked up the phone and made an appointment.

"What's all that junk on your face?" Vera said when she saw Emma at the diner.

"It's makeup." It had taken her four days to be bold enough to wear it outside of her bedroom.

"It looks awful on you. Go and wash it off."

"I think she looks nice," Uncle Lincoln said.

"No use flattering her."

"I'm not." He smiled at his niece and Emma felt her spirits lift. She knew her mother wouldn't approve, but she did feel better about herself. She held her head higher and although most patrons still didn't notice her, she didn't mind. She'd made a new friend. A friend who believed in her.

Emma looked around the diner and her eyes fell on a man she didn't recognize. He looked so sad and lost. She'd never seen him at the diner before. Probably just passing through but she could sense his hurt, she'd seen it in Richard when he'd first arrived, but this man seemed more defeated, more heartbroken, but there was also an element that frightened her...a seething anger.

She walked over to him. "What can I get you?"

"Whatever your specialty is."

She told him.

"I'll take that."

Then Emma took a deep breath and decided to be bold. "We also offer a listening ear. It's sometimes good to share your troubles with a stranger and let them out."

"I'll just take one apple dumpling to go."

"Right," Emma said, feeling foolish. She knew she didn't have the charm of others and he'd shot her down cold.

She went back to the kitchen and gave the order to the cook.

"I don't like the looks of him," her mother said. "At least he doesn't look like a reporter, but you never know."

"Leave him alone, Mother."

"What were you saying to him?"

"I was just being friendly."

"Don't be too friendly. You don't know anything about him."

Emma resisted rolling her eyes. He'd barely given her a second glance. She doubted he'd even remember talking to her. She returned to his table with the food.

"Here you go. And I also made you some tea. It's free and will help to ease your troubles away."

He grunted. "Thanks."

She left him but couldn't keep her eyes off him. She watched him eat and sip the tea. Most customers left the tea untouched, but he'd been bold enough to try it and seemed to like it. That thought made her smile, hoping that the herbs would ease his troubled mind. He looked so troubled and alone. There was something about him that drew her to him. Perhaps because no one paid much attention to him either, but whatever the reason when she saw him go she felt her heart sink as if she'd lost an opportunity.

Daniella wasn't sure what to make of Dr. Brooks. The man she met two weeks later was even more attractive and easygoing than she'd expected. He ushered her into his office and made her feel as welcome as Trenton had made her feel unwelcome. She settled in her chair wondering if she'd gone to the wrong source and as they briefly chatted she sensed that he was genuine.

"Why are you asking about Sheppard again?" Dr. Brooks asked.

"I'm just doing a follow-up on the case. This is merely a formality. How you feel about it after all these years."

"I didn't realize there would be renewed interest."

"There is," Daniella said, seeing the question in his eyes, but determined to be vague.

He shrugged with regret. "I really don't have much to add."

"I'm sure that you do. Your testimony was the most crucial component in the prosecution's case."

"And you want to prove me wrong?"

"Oh, no," she said quickly with a bright smile. "My focus is on the importance of expert testimony in high-profile cases. You can't deny that it was a very hot issue."

"Yes, but as I said I just looked at the findings. *They* were the true witness to the terrible event."

"What did you think about the company Sheldon?"

He paused. "Nothing."

"It's just that Nurse Jones said that they were instrumental in getting things suppressed."

"She doesn't know what she's talking about. And I'm just a doctor. I don't know anything about how the justice system works or what Sheldon's interests were, I just shared my findings."

Daniella nodded. "Thank you for your time."

"Ms. Duvall."

"Daniella, please."

"Daniella. One thing I want your readers to know is that being an expert isn't always easy, especially when someone's life is at stake. It was a very painful case for me. Trenton and I had been close friends and it was hard for me to do what I needed to."

"I'm sure it was. It also makes you more admirable to tell the truth despite the consequences."

"If I were you, I'd let sleeping dogs lie. This case doesn't need to be opened up again. You'll be hurting so many people and you just don't want to do that. Let it go. Go home."

"Funny, Trenton said the same thing."

He blinked. "You spoke to Trenton?"

"Briefly."

"So you know where he is?"

Daniella suddenly knew she should not have offered that bit of information, but Dr. Brooks was beginning to irritate her. Like the others, he was telling her what she should or shouldn't do.

"Sorry, but I can't share that information."

"I'd really like a chance to see him again."

"I'll let him know that."

"You do that. And take my advice. Leave this story alone."

Daniella smiled and left. What had happened to end the friendship between Dr. Brooks and Trenton? Was there a side to Trenton she didn't know? Or another side to Dr. Brooks? She walked into the waiting room with her head lowered, lost in thought, and bumped into someone heading in the opposite direction. She stumbled back and gaped at the woman.

"Oh, I'm sorry," she said, picking up the woman's handbag. Daniella handed it to her and froze. She knew this woman. She'd seen her before but where? She was impeccably dressed in a designer suit and matching stiletto heels.

"It's nothing," the woman said, flashing a gracious smile while retrieving her bag. She walked past and headed straight into Dr. Brooks's office without announcing herself. Obviously she didn't need an appointment. Daniella turned to the front door and then remembered. But it couldn't be. She fished her cell

phone out of her purse and brought up the digital image
of Trenton his father had sent her. And there she was—
the same woman by Trenton's side was now going into
Dr. Brooks's office and acting as if she knew him. Perhaps she did. But how much? Something didn't feel
right. What was Trenton's ex-wife doing with the man
who'd helped topple his career? This new information
was definitely worth looking into.

Fayola Sheppard Brooks walked into her husband's
office and found him standing by the window. "You
look tense, what's wrong?"

"Could be nothing."

She wrapped her arms around his waist. "What?"

He turned to her. "Some woman came around asking about the Sheppard case."

"Why?"

"She gave me a reason, but I don't believe her." She
was up to something, but he wasn't sure what. At least
she knew where Trenton was, and that was good. For
him. But she knew too much. How had she gotten to
Nona? And why was she interested in Sheldon? The
company was now dissolved anyway, so she couldn't
find out too much about them, but still he couldn't let
her make a connection between them. He couldn't let
her ask any more questions.

He was a man who liked to win. And so far he had.
He had the homes, the cars and the wife. He turned to
Fayola. She was definitely a prize worth protecting. She
admired him. Everyone did. He deserved his success.

He'd worked hard to get it and he wouldn't let anyone take it away from him. Besides, he never lost. Never.

He'd make sure that the truth would never be revealed—he couldn't afford it. He'd have to scare her a bit. He could tell she wasn't experienced and he knew people who could be very persuasive. He'd expected to have heard something from Duane by now, but he'd been strangely silent. Perhaps he hadn't gotten him riled up enough. He'd have to find something that would send him over the edge so that he'd take care of Trenton for him once and for all. With this girl and Trenton out of the way, he would finally be able to breathe again.

Emma closed up after a long day at the diner, glad that her shift had ended. It had been a grueling day and she'd made more mistakes than usual, with her mother reminding and berating her for each offense.

"How come you always start dropping things when your mother's around?" her uncle, Lincoln Maxwell Stone, had asked her as she cleaned up the spill from a glass she'd let slip off her tray. She'd been thankful the glass had been plastic.

Emma shrugged. She always felt comfortable with her uncle, but didn't know how to answer him. "I wish I knew, but I don't. I'm sorry, I guess I'm just clumsy."

"No, you're not, she just makes you think you are. That's how she sees you and that's how you've started to see yourself."

"Because it's true."

Her uncle shook his head. "No, it's not. I've watched you all your life and when your mother isn't around you're quick and free. I watched the care you take when making tea or garnishing a dish. But the moment Vera shows up, you're all thumbs."

Emma stared at him, amazed. "Really?"

"Yes."

"I never knew that."

"It's the truth. I think it happens because you're trying too hard to please her. I understand. I worked hard to please my parents, too, but there comes a time when you have to stop. And you're old enough to stop now."

"But I've never pleased her, how can I stop trying? I still hope that one day I'll do something that will make her proud of me."

"How long are you planning to wait for that day? Emma, we're not given infinite time to live on this earth. We're all just hourglasses that will one day run out. You have to decide where you want to be when your time comes."

"That sounds morbid."

"It's true. Your father left us far too soon with a long list of things he'd wanted to do but was too afraid to try. I don't want that for you. Vera is a hard woman to please. I know, I grew up with her. You need to start learning to please yourself."

Emma remembered her uncle's words as she headed to her car. She was old enough to stop trying to please her mother. She was old enough to start believing in herself and follow her heart. She looked up and saw a pink and purple sky while a sparrow sitting on top of the roof of the diner sang out. She inhaled the soft evening breeze and smiled.

"Hey!" a voice called.

Emma jumped, spun around and saw the man from the diner.

"I didn't mean to scare you," he said quickly, his hands held out in apology. "Thanks for the tea."

"You're welcome."

"My name is Duane and I was just wondering if that listening ear was still on the menu?"

Emma's heart lifted. He'd come back. This was her chance. "Yes. There's a library not far from here and—"

"Emma!"

She spun around and saw her mother approaching, carrying two medium-sized boxes. "Excuse me." She rushed over to her. "Yes?"

"I need your help."

Emma glanced at Duane. "I'm busy."

Vera raised her voice. "You'd choose to help some stranger over me?"

"Quiet."

"That's okay," Duane said, beginning to walk away.

Her heart sank. "No, really."

"Perhaps another time," he said then headed for his car.

Vera handed Emma the boxes. "Good, he's gone."

"Mom, these boxes are empty," Emma said, exasperated.

"I had to stop you from making a fool of yourself."

Emma dropped the boxes. "Mother."

"You put a little rouge on your face and then suddenly go after the first man that looks at you?"

"He just wanted to talk."

"I told you he's no good. There's something fishy about him."

"You can't tell that just by looking at someone."

"I can. Now help me with these boxes."

Emma shook her head. "What am I supposed to do with them?"

"Put them back where I found them."

Emma sighed then did what her mother said.

Duane gripped his steering wheel. He would have liked someone to talk to tonight instead of going to his room alone. He'd gotten sick of his own company and the deep recesses of his thoughts. What was he doing here? He'd been crazy to come and try to face Sheppard. He should just go home and travel some more. Revenge never helped anyone.

He glanced down when his cell phone rang. At first he hoped it was Emma saying they could talk after all, then he remembered that she didn't have his number.

"Hello?"

"Have you seen Sheppard yet?" Dr. Brooks asked.

"No," he said, surprised by the urgency in the doctor's voice. "Look, I don't—"

"I just found out some more news. He's getting married."

Duane felt the blood leave him as if he'd been sucked dry. "Married?"

"Yes. Soon."

"When?"

Duane felt his heart painfully constrict when he heard the date. It was the same day Latisha had died.

Her face rose up in his mind, then he remembered seeing her lying in the coffin. "No."

"Yes, that date doesn't mean anything to him. He's moving on with his life. He'll probably soon start a family. You and Latisha had wanted to start a family, right?"

"Yes," he said, his voice weak.

"But that can never happen now. Sheppard doesn't care about what happened, but it's up to you to make him care. Face your fears or you'll always feel this way," he said, then disconnected.

Duane felt his rage build. How could Sheppard get married again? Find love? Be happy? How could he live the life he'd stolen away from him? No, he could never rest until Sheppard suffered the way he had. He'd been right to come. He would confront him and make sure his face was the last one Sheppard ever saw.

Two more pieces to the puzzle, Daniella thought as she drove back to Sykesville. Dr. Brooks knew Trenton and knew him well. She sensed he was hiding something, but what? She'd seen a slight sheen of sweat when she referred to his testimony but more so when he mentioned Sheldon and the suppressed lab work. Guilt, remorse or something else? And what was Fayola doing there? Excitement raced up her spine. Maybe this bit of information was something she could use to persuade Trenton that she could help him.

Evening was descending in a blaze of color as Daniella drove into town. She parked her car in the parking lot of the bed-and-breakfast and locked up. She was about to grab her laptop from the trunk when someone put a cover over her head. She had no chance to scream as two men bound her hands and legs. Soon she felt herself being lifted up and set into a trunk. *This isn't happening,* she thought, feeling panicked. She could hear the gravel crunch beneath her as the car sped down the road. She tried to loosen her hands and feet, but nothing budged. She kicked the trunk door, hoping to knock out a taillight, but before she could succeed, the car slowed to a stop. She heard the trunk door lift and the same pairs of hands lifted her up and walked a few yards before unceremoniously dropping her on the ground. She felt the hood lift, but it didn't help much. The two men had their faces covered, only exposing their eyes and mouth. One man put tape over her mouth, preventing her from screaming out.

"This is a warning. Go home. If you don't, one of your sisters will suffer a very tragic accident."

The man who spoke flashed a cold smile and turned. He had a slim build with dirty nails and a coarse-looking jacket. The other man walked toward her. She could tell he liked expensive shoes, he wore an expensive pair made of snakeskin. Fear, stark and vivid, coursed through her. She sensed what was on his mind.

When the first man didn't sense his companion following, he turned. "What are you doing?"

The second man kneeled down and grabbed Daniella's chin and pulled off the tape from around her mouth. "She's a good-looking woman. I've always wondered what it'd be like making love to a beautiful woman." He ran his hand over her thigh. She winced at his touch, but he didn't care. "We could have fun with her."

"That's not what we're here for."

"She even smells good. I'd consider it a bonus." He yanked her forward and pressed his thick, cracked lips on hers.

The other man grabbed him and roughly lifted him up. "It's too risky. If your mask falls off we'd have to kill her."

"So what? No one will find her out here."

"When I kill, I don't leave witnesses."

The second man swore and shook his head. "What a waste," he said. "Wait, we're going to just leave her out here?"

"Just long enough for our message to get through."

"Shouldn't we at least cover her? The temperatures drop out here in the mountains and—"

"When did you become a mother hen? I'm the one in charge here. She'll be fine when we come back to get her."

"I won't say anything," Daniella said, trying to hide the fear in her voice. "If you'd just loosen my hands."

The slender man knelt in front of her, close enough for her to see his eyes. "Lady, I want to believe you."

"You can trust me. I promise I won't tell anyone."

His eyes were hollow and without feeling. She knew she'd get no kindness from him. "Sorry."

He stood and the two men left. Soon a light drizzle began to fall.

Daniella rested her head back on the dry leaves beneath her, trying to still her heart. She knew their voices at least, but that wouldn't be enough. First she had to get out of there. She rubbed her trapped wrists against the tree desperate to get loose. Although it was the middle of spring, with relatively warm temperatures during the day, exposure to the cool wind and rain that had started falling during the night caused Daniella's body temperature to drop quickly. And unfortunately, the clothes she was wearing were inadequate, putting her at risk of hypothermia, if she didn't get out of there soon.

The night before, when she was packing in anticipation of driving back to Sykesville and staying at the bed-and-breakfast for several days, she had made sure to include enough outfits in her suitcase to cover whatever situation she found herself in. She'd included several new negligees she had purchased at Bloomingdale's, just in case she decided to take Trenton up on his offer. She hadn't planned on doing any hiking, but on a whim, had decided to include a pair of boots, several pairs of wool socks and a lightweight jacket. But she hadn't planned on being left out in the elements with her hands and feet bound.

She was so cold her entire body started to shiver. She lay on the ground, wondering if anyone would hear her if she cried out, and wishing she had been wearing her jacket. Unfortunately, whenever she got in her car, one of the things she always did was take off her jacket or coat.

She found wearing them and putting on a seat belt over them too stifling, and besides, she always used the car heater to keep her warm. She had traveled the entire distance wearing just a pair of jeans, a short-sleeved, silk-cashmere top, a pair of running shoes and no socks. She was freezing. She felt wet and cold. After struggling unsuccessfully to undo the duct tape, she was exhausted. All she wanted to do was go to sleep. She paused when she heard footsteps. She glanced up and saw the first man, she could tell by his build, walking toward her.

"I can't let you see which direction we go in," he said pulling out a gun.

"I can't see the road," Daniella said, panicked. "I won't see where you go."

He nodded. "That's right. I'm going to make sure." He lifted the gun in his hand. "Sweet dreams."

Daniella felt pain explode in her head then darkness.

Nine-year-old Joel Wells and his best friend, Gary Hayford, loved the woods. There was so much to do and explore. They saw a doe with two fawns dart past and the red flash of a fox while a gray squirrel raced up a tree with leaves in its mouth.

"Hey, what's that?" Gary said, pointing to something in the distance.

"I don't know," Joel said, cautiously stepping closer. "Let's get a better look."

Gary rushed ahead, bolder than his friend. "This is gonna be cool! My cousin once found a mountain bike that had been dumped and we fixed it up good."

"Yeah, you can find a lot of things out here," Joel said, gaining courage. "My aunt caught Regina and Juan out here once going at it. Boy did they get it. If it's them again—" He abruptly halted and froze.

Gary turned to his friend, confused. "What is it? Why did you stop?"

"I know what it is. It's a dead body."

Chapter 9

There was an emergency. Trenton's radio, which he always kept on, had picked up the signal. A couple of young boys hiking high in the mountains had come upon a body. They had used their cell phone to dial 911 and call for help. Trenton didn't wait to be notified by the emergency 911 call center, which was the usual process. From the information he was able to get over the radio, he knew that his property was close to where the boys said they were. He took off in his truck to save time, instead of going to the fire station in town to get one of the town's two emergency vehicles. This was a common practice of his. Major medical emergencies were so infrequent that Trenton kept his truck equipped to deal with anything that came along.

On his way to the scene, he called the fire station and let the fire chief, Regan Hayman, know that he was on his way and had the situation under control. As a trained medic pilot and EMT, Chief Hayman knew he had nothing to worry about. Trenton told him that once he was on the scene, he'd let him know what the situation was and whether or not he needed additional assistance. Both men agreed that although the caller said they had found a body, that it was likely just someone playing around and nothing to really worry about. They'd had several pranks like that before.

It took Trenton less than five minutes to arrive at the location. In the dying light, his headlights illuminated the two young boys wildly jumping up and down and pointing off to the side. Trenton turned to the right, and drove a short distance before spotting a body lying still on the ground. He jumped out, grabbed his emergency backpack and ran over to the victim. As he got closer, his heart began racing. He recognized the lifeless body before him. It was Daniella with her hands and feet bound. What was she doing here?

"Dear God, who did this to you?" he said, knowing there would be no reply.

He thought she had gone home. The night before she left, she had called his house to let him know that she "wasn't going to give up that easily." He hadn't replied. It wasn't the message he had been waiting for. He had been waiting for an invitation to spend the night. The next day, he'd checked the bed-and-breakfast, just to make sure she had left and the owner, Ms. Swiftlog, a nosy busybody, had given him a minute-by-minute account of everything Daniella did before driving off in her car.

When had she returned? Why had she returned? But he knew there was no time for questions, and he quickly changed gears. He assured the two boys that they could leave and he would take it from there. He called one of the boys' parents who said they would be there to pick them up. It was getting late and darkness was settling quickly around them, despite the longer spring days. The parents had been relieved to hear from him since they'd expected the boys home by dinnertime.

However, knowing that the news of the woman in the woods would spread faster than an oil slick, Trenton assured the boys and their parents that he knew the young lady, she was a friend of his, and must have fallen and hit her head. As a result, she was only unconscious not dead. The boys nodded but Trenton knew they were eager to run off and the spread the news about the mystery woman they'd found in the woods.

Trenton could see from Daniella's condition that she needed immediate medical attention.

He sprang into action. He had to get Daniella into his vehicle fast to prevent any further heat loss, which was critical. It didn't appear that her hypothermia was severe, or she would have ceased shivering. Because she was unconscious, he couldn't assess whether she had slurred speech, confusion or loss of memory, which were signs of severe hypothermia. What he needed to do now was to shield her body from any further exposure to cold. He decided against taking her to the hospital, which was about forty minutes away or calling the local doctor in town. He was a kind man, but hadn't grown much in his profession and Trenton knew he knew more about medicine and emergency care than the doctor did anyway. He had the situation under control.

He called Chief Regan and downgraded her condition, to avoid contributing to the rumor mill. He let Regan know that she was a friend of his and he'd take care of her minor injuries. Fire Chief Regan was happy to have Trenton as part of his emergency personnel, which consisted of himself, two firefighters, an ambulance driver and Trenton, the EMT. Besides, it was a Saturday night, and he felt relieved that he didn't have to miss his weekly card game at the local community hall.

Trenton settled Daniella inside his truck then sped down the road, only missing driving straight into his house by about a foot. Layla jumped out of the way as Trenton barged into the house carrying Daniella's unconscious body in his arms. He leaped up the steps, three at a time, and gently placed her on his bed. He couldn't put her in the shower, it would be hard holding her up and having her lie down in the stall wouldn't work and he didn't have a bathtub. The house had been built as a vacation hideaway. It had a bedroom loft, with a small bathroom that consisted of a toilet, wash bowl and a primitive shower. He went into his closet and pulled out an electric blanket and plugged it in. He set it on warm. He knew that putting a person with hyperthermia under anything hot, like hot water, could be disastrous. Before putting her under the blanket, he cut off her wet clothing, leaving her underwear on, hoping she wouldn't sue him once she recovered. He remembered one call he had been on, where a woman had been involved in a car accident, and in order to get her out safely, they had to cut her fur jacket and pair of leather pants. They saved the woman's life only to have her sue the fire department for damages. But loss of her clothing was of no concern to him at the moment.

He needed to warm the center of her body. He used the electric blanket, which was king-size, to wrap her snugly inside. As her body temperature started to increase, he was able to extend it to include her head and neck. He checked on her every fifteen minutes, not wanting to leave her side. Time passed by slowly. Layla watched him pace. As soon as Daniella began to regain consciousness, Trenton had her sip some warm herbal tea, grateful that he had some on hand because of Vera. He wanted to get Daniella to eat a small amount of some sweet, high carbohydrate snacks he had, to provide energy to help her keep warm, but Daniella, although no longer unconscious, was still not totally coherent and he didn't want to risk her choking on something. He monitored her for any breathing or cardiovascular problems. There was none and there was no sign of frostbite. Thankfully she hadn't been out in the open for too long. Again, the questions returned. Why was she there? Why or when had she returned? Who had done this to her?

Daniella began to turn, and Trenton noticed her raising her hand to her head. He gently examined her head, probing as tenderly as possible and discovered that whoever had kidnapped and tied her up, had also pistol-whipped her and left her out there to die. If the two boys hadn't found her, in several more days she would not have been found alive.

"Ouch! That hurts."

"Hold still, I need to clean the area." He parted her hair and discovered a large gash that needed to be cleaned and closed with a few stitches. Damn. He didn't have any anesthesia; he'd have to close it without numbing the area. He'd have to do it quickly. He noticed that the side of her face was beginning to swell and a nasty purplish-blue bruise was starting to show. From what he saw upon examining her, she had sustained quite a beating. Anger began to rise in him, but he fought to push it aside because he needed a cool head to perform the task he had to do. Once he'd finished stitching her up, he sat by her side as she slept.

What had he done? He had stayed out of hiding to protect himself. He had no idea that being visible would have led to something like this. Why? He knew this woman was just trying to get his story, but she hadn't written anything yet. So, who was trying to kill her and why? Maybe his hunch was true. He looked at Daniella again. She finally looked peaceful, thanks to several sleeping pills he had put in her tea. Why was this beautiful woman being targeted like this? He knew he had to do something. Murder or intimidation had never been on his mind. He had accepted his fate and was lying low, creating a new identity and starting a new life. Now it was time for him to figure out what was going on. Trenton Sheppard was no longer going to hide, he would bury Richard Engleright and come alive once more.

She couldn't scream, she couldn't cry out. Nobody could help her. Her mind was a blur of dark masks, Trenton's hand, his voice, the sound of a cold, relentless drizzle soaking through her clothes. She thought of her sister Mariella warning her about heading into danger. This was the second time she'd faced death, another terrifying time in the woods, but there had been no Trenton to save her…but wait, he had been there. She remembered flashes of him. His arms, his voice. Or perhaps it had all been her imagination. Those two men would come back to get her and—

"Shh…" a deep, soothing voice said. "You're safe now."

Daniella opened her eyes and saw Trenton beside her and Layla sleeping at her feet. She felt the warmth and comfort they offered and promptly burst into tears.

Trenton gathered her close. He didn't ask her any questions, for which she was grateful. A part of her was still terrified it was all just a dream and that she would wake up alone in the woods with her arms and legs bound and left to die.

"I won't let anyone hurt you," he said. "Who did this?"

"I don't know. I didn't see their faces."

"Who did you talk to?"

"What?"

"Before this happened. Who did you talk to?"

"Um…your parents, a nurse, Dr. Brooks—"

He swore.

"You think he did this?"

"I don't know, but—" He shook his head. "Damn it, Daniella. I told you to go home."

"I just wanted to help you."

His patience snapped. He stood. "You call this help-ing me? Getting yourself nearly killed?"

She tried to hold back tears, but he saw them swim-ming in her eyes anyway and sighed. "I'm sorry. I didn't mean to shout, but I nearly lost you. What would I have done then?"

"Will you let me help you now?"

"I should pack you up and drive you directly to where you live myself." He turned on the radio.

She frowned. "Is that country?"

He shot her a glance. "Do you have something against country?"

"No," she said quickly. "I was just asking."

"Hmm."

"Are you going to stay angry with me?"

"Do you expect me to applaud you?" Trenton looked at her for a long moment. He knew he was going to re-gret this, but he had no other choice but to find out what she knew. She'd gotten in too deep and he had to get her out of it. The only way to do that was to keep an eye on her. He'd underestimated her stubbornness. Just what he needed—someone else to worry about. Layla had had another of her attacks last night and now he had to deal with a delusional woman who felt it was her duty to save him. "Tell me everything you know."

"I don't know much yet."

"Someone thinks you do."

"I saw Fayola."

He paused. "Where?"

"In Dr. Brooks's office."

Trenton stared at her for a long moment then fell on

the bed and covered his face. "I shouldn't be surprised. I am, but I shouldn't be." He swore.

Daniella lightly touched his arm, feeling helpless to relieve his pain. "I'm sorry."

His shoulders tensed and his jaw twitched. "It's not your fault. She found someone better."

"You still love her?"

Trenton let his hands fall, defeated. "Does it matter now?"

No, it didn't. She changed the subject. "He's hiding something. And…"

He shook his head.

"The lab results were suppressed. I spoke to—"

"I don't care," he said, his voice hollow.

"You did a minute ago."

"That was different."

"That was before I told you about Fayola."

He turned away.

"I'm sorry you had hopes of getting back together, but I need you to care about the truth because it matters. Please don't let my ordeal be for nothing. You can't give up."

"Why not?" He tapped his chest. "What do you want from me? Why do you want me to be the man that I'm not?"

"I want a chance to repay you."

"I don't need it."

"I came after you for selfish reasons. I wanted to show Pascal that I could do investigative journalism. I wanted to tell your story for my own glory and I'm ashamed of that now. I realized that I don't want to be the woman Pascal dared me to be. Digging into your past, hurting people is not the kind of legacy I want to leave. I need to feel valuable. I need to believe my life was really worth saving."

"It is."

"You don't understand. What have I really done with my life? Nothing. If I'd died my family would have missed me, but that's it. I didn't do anything great. I've never really done anything impulsive. At least not on my own," she said to correct herself, thinking of the challenge she and her sisters had come up with to catch a man. "I lived for myself and it was easy and fun. But I'm not that woman anymore. You saved my life and now I'm going to save yours."

"Okay, tell me more."

Daniella told him everything and he listened then hung his head when she was through. "This much we know. They wanted to scare you because they left you alive. If you stop asking questions, maybe whoever did this will relax and not worry. You need to stay safe. You'll lie low here for a few days and then we'll start again. Fortunately, we have time. We can use that time to let him get comfortable again. I need him to drop his guard."

"Okay, what should we do now?"

"Sleep."

"Oh," she said in a quiet tone, the room suddenly becoming more intimate. She was in his domain and she quickly realized how vulnerable she was to him. "You have another bedroom?"

"No, but I'll be a gentleman and sleep on the couch."

"You don't have to."

He paused. His voice caught. "What do you mean?"

"You can stay here."

Trenton laughed. "I'm not that much of a gentleman."

"But I don't want to be alone."

He pointed. "I'm just down the hall and there's Layla."

"Please," she pleaded.

Trenton rested his hands on his hips then released a fierce sigh. "All right." He brushed his teeth, changed into his boxers, turned off the lights then got in the bed. He stiffened when she snuggled up against him. "Wait, what are you doing?"

"Keeping warm."

"You need an extra blanket?"

"Not if you hold me."

He groaned. "I can't hold you."

"You did before."

"That was different."

"Please."

"Daniella—"

"Pretty please?"

He was silent a moment then said, "Fine. Five minutes." He drew her close then looked at his watch. "Starting now."

"I'm glad you're the one who found me."

"Hmm."

"At first I thought I was dreaming." She snuggled closer, rubbing her cheek against his chest. He was hard, warm and smooth, just as she'd hoped he'd be. "Who would have thought you were so cuddly?"

"I'm not cuddly," he grumbled.

"Yes, you are—so warm and tender and—"

His voice deepened. "Stop moving like that."

"I can't help it, it feels so good. I wish this moment could last forever."

Trenton jumped out of the bed. "Okay, time's up."

He left and minutes later, Daniella heard the shower turn on. She fell asleep with a smile on her face. At least he wouldn't be thinking about Fayola tonight.

Trenton didn't think about Fayola at all. A cold shower didn't help either. He wrapped a towel around himself and went downstairs to the kitchen where he grabbed a bag of popcorn and then he went to the couch and watched TV until he drifted off to sleep.

"What do you mean you left her in the woods?" Dr. Brooks said.

"Just to frighten her."

"You were supposed to scare her not kill her. She could die from exposure out there in the mountains."

"Don't worry, Doc. When we drove back there she was gone," he said, not wanting to admit that he'd forgotten about her because he'd spent some of his money on drugs and a hot whore with a name he still couldn't pronounce.

"Are you sure she didn't know who you are?" Brooks said.

"Positive. She was real scared. Near tears. You don't have to worry about her anymore."

Chapter 10

Trenton woke to the smell of smoke. He jumped up and headed to the kitchen where he found Daniella opening the windows and waving away black billows of smoke. She was wearing his robe. It was too big for her but he liked what he saw. He glanced at a burnt pan lying in the sink.

"What happened?"

She turned to him then quickly dropped her gaze, embarrassed. "Sorry, I didn't mean to wake you."

He walked over to the sink. "What were you trying to make?"

"Breakfast."

"We can just go into town."

"I wasn't sure you'd want to be seen with me."

"Why not?"

"People will talk."

"People are already talking. Eating together won't make a difference." He poured himself a glass of orange juice.

The doorbell rang.

He set his glass down. "I'll get it."

Daniella flew at him and blocked his path. "No!"

He halted. "What?"

"You can't answer the door."

"Richard?" a voice called.

He groaned. "It's Vera. Don't worry, I can get rid of her. At least for a while." He took a step around her.

Daniella jumped in front of him again and tried to push him back. "Are you crazy? You can't answer it. She'll talk."

He frowned. "She'll talk anyway. She knows I'm here. In a minute she'll peek through the window."

Daniella threw her arms around him and glanced behind her. "Shouldn't you close the blinds?"

"There's nothing to see." He stared down at her, confused. "I'm not saying I'm not enjoying this, but what's wrong with you?"

"Don't you care?"

He gently, but firmly, unlatched her arms. "No, I can handle Vera."

Daniella rushed in front of him again. "Not like this. Look at you."

He glanced down then glanced over at the couch where his towel from last night still lay. "Oh. That explains why you felt so good against me." He glanced up and waved at Vera who was peering through the window. Daniella blocked her full view of him. She turned and remained in front of him. "We'll be right there," she called to her.

Vera nodded then went to the front door.

Daniella turned to Trenton. "Go put something on."

"Wearing you seems to be working." He narrowed his gaze. "Actually, I have a better idea." He reached for her robe.

She grasped the collar. "What are you doing?"

"I'll just put this on."

"You can't."

He frowned. "Why not?"

"It was going to be a surprise after breakfast."

"A surprise?"

"Yes."

A slow, sensuous smile spread on his face. "You mean you're not wearing anything underneath?"

"No."

"You can surprise me now."

"There's Vera."

He furrowed his brows as if she'd said a foreign word. "Vera?"

"Yes, she's at the door."

He nodded as if suddenly remembering. "Oh, right, her. I'll get it."

Daniella grabbed his arm. "You forgot your towel."

"Oh." He quickly grabbed the towel, wrapping it around his waist and headed for the door then stopped and pointed at Daniella. "Promise not to change your mind."

"About what?"

"My surprise."

She grinned, briefly baring her shoulder before hiding it under the robe again. "I won't, just answer the door."

Trenton stared at her while he fumbled for the door handle.

Daniella covered her mouth to keep from laughing then said, "Do you need help?"

Trenton turned to the door. "No, I'm fine," he said then opened the door and welcomed Vera inside. "Sorry to have kept you waiting, Vera."

"That's okay," she said, giving him an odd look then sending a suspicious glance Daniella's way. Then she sniffed the air. "What's that awful smell?" she said heading for the kitchen.

"I was making breakfast," Daniella said.

Vera looked at the burnt remnants. "My Emma knows how to cook."

"So does Daniella," Trenton lied. "It's my fault, I distracted her."

"Oh. Well, I brought you a few things. You love Emma's deviled eggs, don't you, Trenton?"

Trenton didn't reply. He was too busy staring at Daniella with a big grin on his face, like a child who knew he was about to open the perfect birthday present. Daniella couldn't help grinning back.

"Richard?" Vera snapped.

He blinked and looked at her. "Huh?"

"You didn't hear a word I said, did you?"

"No," he said flatly.

Vera set the rest of the items on the counter and

turned to Daniella. "I heard you got attacked. What were you doing out in the woods all by yourself?"

"That wasn't her," Trenton said.

"The description certainly sounded like her."

"It wasn't. She was with me."

"Oh." She measured Daniella with a cool look. "Fine. I was just looking to see that you were okay, but I guess I didn't need to." She walked past him to the front door. "Sorry to have bothered you."

"Me, too," he said then winced when Daniella hit him. "I mean, thanks." He ushered her out the door. "There goes my free meals. I will miss their cooking." He turned to Daniella and rubbed his hands in anticipation. "Surprise time." He reached out for her.

"Wait," she said, holding him off. "Not yet." She turned.

He grabbed the belt of her robe, stopping her. "You promised not to change your mind."

"I haven't changed my mind. I just thought this would be better upstairs."

"Why not here? No one's looking."

"Upstairs or no surprise."

Trenton sighed, resigned, then grabbed her hand. "Okay, you win," he said, running up the stairs and dragging her behind him. He raced into the bedroom, lifted her onto the bed then rested his hands on his hips. "Better now?"

"Almost." Daniella jumped down from the bed and pulled out a condom from her robe pocket. "First I have to check and make sure you're ready."

"Honey—" his voice broke into huskiness "—I'm more than ready."

"I want to find out for myself," she said, slipping her hand underneath his towel. She stroked the inside of his thigh, surprised by how smooth and firm he felt. He was definitely a well-made man. She then wrapped her fingers around him. "You're getting there," she teased.

His eyes caught and held hers. "I'm as hard as a pole."

"Let me be the judge of that." She opened the condom then pulled off his towel.

He lifted a mocking brow. "Convinced yet?"

"Almost. Just one more test."

"Test?" Trenton's voice cracked with impatience. "I'm waiting for my surprise."

"It's coming."

He reached for her again. "I want it now."

Daniella stepped out of reach. "Here it is." She let the robe slide to the ground then she put the condom in her mouth and got down on her knees and began rolling it on, stopping halfway.

"What's wrong?" Trenton glanced down at her.

Daniella cleared her throat without looking up. "You're more than I expected," she said, rolling the rest of the condom on with her hand.

"You haven't done this before?"

"I have, I just…you're more than a mouthful. I haven't had to deal with so…" She let her words fade away.

"Much?" Trenton finished.

Daniella felt her face grow warm. "Size doesn't matter."

Trenton reached his hand down and raised her chin,

forcing her to look at him, his tone playful. "It does if you know how to use it to your advantage."

"Then you have a big advantage!" She glanced down. "You're as hard as a rocket."

"Ready for takeoff."

"Good." Daniella moved in front of him, turned, then bent over, tossing him an inviting smile over her shoulder. "Then take me to the moon."

He took her there and back. At one point he took her off her feet. She thought she'd never come down ever again. It was pure pleasure—explosive and dynamic—and it filled her, soaring higher and higher. They both collapsed on the ground.

"That was incredible," Trenton said, slightly out of breath.

Daniella could only nod. She'd never had three orgasms in a row; her body felt so alive, as if she could float up to the ceiling. She never knew lovemaking could be so exciting. Fun? Yes. Enjoyable? Definitely. But this was mind-altering. She wasn't sure she knew herself anymore.

Trenton turned on his side and let his hand trail a sensuous path down her stomach to her center. He closed his eyes and sighed in ecstasy. "Pure silk." He rubbed his cheek against her skin, his breath making her flesh tingle. "I haven't felt silk in such a long time."

Daniella laughed. "Silk? Open your eyes. I'm not wearing anything."

"I know." He lifted his head, his smoldering gaze meeting hers. "Your body is silk to me." His mouth covered hers and soon he was inside her again sending ripples of erotic delight cascading over her like a wave. He took her beyond the moon to another galaxy and when they were through they again collapsed, but this time in each other's arms.

Daniella traced his earlobe with her finger. "You were right."

"About what?"

"You know how to use it."

"I've never used it like that before. You bring out something in me."

"You do the same to me, all of my inhibitions melt away."

Trenton laughed and cupped her bottom. "With me, they'll always disappear."

Daniella drew her lips close to Trenton's ear and whispered, "We'll have to try this a few more times before that can happen."

"I'll be happy to help you." He squeezed her bottom. "After I've eaten something."

"You're hungry?"

"I'm starving."

Daniella sat up. "Okay, let's eat." She stood and grabbed the robe.

He took it from her. "No, you don't need that."

"You want me to eat naked?"

"Why not? Don't get shy on me now."

"I just— I've never made breakfast naked before."

"There's a first time for everything. Besides, you don't have to cook anything. I have a fridge full of cooked food, all we have to do is heat it up. I'll do that."

He pulled her up to her feet. She winced. He paused. "What's wrong?"

She touched the side of her face. "My head's a little sore, that's all," she said, surprised she hadn't felt anything while they were making love.

Trenton swore. "I'm so sorry. I forgot."

Daniella smiled, wanting to reassure him. "I'm fine, really. Just be gentle with me."

"I will," he said, making it sound like a vow. Trenton went into the bathroom and came out holding a glass of water and some pain medicine. Then he lifted her weightlessly into his arms and carried her downstairs and placed her on a chair in the kitchen.

Daniella stood.

He frowned. "What are you doing?"

"I want to help you."

"You should rest."

"I don't need to rest."

He pointed to the kitchen cabinets. "Set the table then."

She grabbed some plates and laid them out and then the cutlery and waited. Minutes later Trenton came over to the table with scrambled eggs, pancakes and syrup. She fixed her plate then started eating. She glanced up and saw Trenton with his chin in his hand watching her with a silly grin on his face.

"Trenton?"

"Yea?"

"Stop staring."

His grin widened. "I can't help it. I had a dream like

this once. Of course I was eating off you, but we'll try that another time."

"You're embarrassing me."

"Consider it a compliment." His gaze landed on her breasts like a tangible caress, her entire body grew hot.

She filled his plate. "Eat something."

His gaze trailed the length of her. "If I could eat you up, I'd never be hungry again."

She stood and walked past him. "I'm putting a robe on."

He grabbed her wrist. "Okay I'll stop or at least I'll try to." He pulled her onto his lap then dumped her plate on top of his.

"What are you doing?"

"We can eat from the same plate." He scooped up some eggs and ate.

She did, too. She loved having him close, vastly aware of their differences and delighting in each of them—from his pebble-hard nipples, his ripped chest and muscular arms.

"Who's Pascal?" Trenton asked.

"The man I thought I would marry one day."

"Hmm."

"He's my ex-boyfriend. He's also the reason why I'm here. He encouraged me to write your story."

"I should call and thank him," he teased.

After breakfast they decided to go for a walk. On their return, Layla had a seizure. After it had passed, Daniella knelt down and stroked her. She looked up at Trenton. "What's wrong with her?"

"A brain tumor, but the surgery will cost eight thousand dollars."

"Did you get a second opinion?"

He looked at her blankly.

"You didn't even think about it."

"He's the top vet in the area and I wouldn't want to cause bad feelings by…"

"This is Layla's life. You need to be certain that such a radical surgery is necessary. I can take her for a second opinion if you don't want anyone to find out."

"It will be the same diagnosis."

"Let's still check. I'll look around and make an appointment."

"You can put it under my name."

"Which one?"

He took a deep breath, realizing that he could no longer hide. It was time to come out of the shadows starting now. "Trenton Sheppard."

The first person in town Trenton revealed his real identity to was Chief Regan, who didn't care, but others weren't so cavalier when they learned the truth. A third of the town believed in his innocence, another third thought he was guilty, and the last third didn't care one way or the other. The third that cared stopped talking when Trenton walked into the diner. He sat at the counter prepared for Vera to ignore him.

She didn't.

"So what they're saying is true? You've been living under an assumed name 'cause you killed some woman?"

"I didn't kill her."

"No, you don't look like a killer to me. I believe you." She glanced at a customer who was scowling at them. "And anyone who has a problem with that can go eat elsewhere," she announced loudly. The customer grumbled under his breath, but turned away.

"Are you here to see Emma?" she asked hopefully.

"No, actually, I wanted to talk to your brother."

"He's in back. You can go round and see him."

"Thanks." Trenton walked to Lincoln's office located at the rear of the diner and knocked on the door.

"Come in."

Trenton walked in, unsure if Lincoln would be as understanding as his sister had been. "Hey."

Lincoln greeted him with a warm smile, melting away his apprehension. "Engleright." He suddenly frowned. "Oh, wait, it's Sheppard now, isn't it?"

"Yes, I had my reasons."

Lincoln held up his hands. "Which are none of my business. I always thought Engleright was a funny name."

Trenton took a seat in one of Lincoln's worn chairs. "I could use your help."

Lincoln leaned forward on his desk, intrigued. "What do you need?"

"You are the eyes of the community. Plus, I know that you and Ms. Swiftlog at the B and B are uh…close," Trenton said, aware that Lincoln and the B and B owner were an item.

"The woman's a busybody," Lincoln said with a knowing grin. "But when she's not running her mouth or spreading gossip, we're at it like rabbits. I have no shame in admitting it."

Trenton laughed at his honesty. "Glad to hear it."

"From what I've heard from Vera, I'm not the only one getting lucky."

Trenton feigned innocence. "I don't know what you mean."

Lincoln only shook his head. "What can I do for you?"

"I wanted to know if either of you noticed any strangers coming through. Did you see anyone who looked suspicious?"

"I didn't, but Helen saw a car waiting in the parking lot of the bed-and-breakfast. She said she didn't like how it was just sitting seeming to wait so she took down the license plate just in case she needed to call the police or get it towed."

Trenton nodded. "Good. I'll need the license. Anything more you can tell me?"

"Around the same time I saw a skinny black guy come in here with eyes like hollowed-out wood. He just asked for a glass of water then left. But he gave me the creeps, Emma and Vera, too."

"Yes, he has that effect on people."

"You know him?"

"I think we have a mutual acquaintance."

"Be careful—he seemed dangerous."

Trenton stood. "When I'm through with him, he won't be dangerous anymore."

Minutes later Trenton left the diner with a license plate number and a plan. He knew the man Lincoln had described. He'd met him before: L.Z. A lifelong criminal known only by his initials. He'd been arrested at Brooks's office for burglary but for some reason Brooks had dropped the charges. Evidently Brooks had found another use for him. Trenton would track him down and find out more and then make him pay for what he'd done to Daniella. He'd just have to remind himself not to kill him.

Daniella couldn't stop smiling. She absently made an appointment for Layla and also did more research on Dr. Brooks, but her mind wandered about the night before. Her phone rang. She glanced down at the number and quickly snapped back into reality—it was Pascal.

"Hello?"

"Thank God," he said with feeling. "I've been trying to reach you for days. I was worried something had happened."

"Oh, something did. It seems there were lab inconsistencies with his case that I'm going to look into further. Trenton will be vindicated, I'm sure of it."

"Good, but you haven't sent me any more of your work."

"Because I'm not doing the story."

"What?"

"I'm doing the investigation for him. If he wants to tell his story, fine, but I won't tell it for him."

Pascal sighed. "I should have known you'd fall for him."

"It's more than that. My priorities have shifted."

"You've worked too hard to let it all go to waste."

"It won't. You'll see. Besides, I'm lying low for a while because I think the doctor's involved. In a few weeks we'll check into his records."

"Good luck."

"Thanks." Daniella went back to her research then took some time to take Layla for another walk.

When Trenton returned from work, he handed Daniella a large store bag.

"I got your bag from your car, but I also bought you some clothes," he said.

"Oh, good, I was going to ask you about that." She shuffled the items inside. "Wait a minute. This is all underwear."

"I thought I should just focus on the basics."

Daniella pulled out a lace and silk pantie.

"Hope they fit."

"Where did you buy these? I know you didn't get these in town."

"There's a place," he said mysteriously.

"You must have driven far."

"It was worth the drive."

She pulled out a silver trimmed garter belt.

He grinned. "Especially that one."

She shook her head and laughed. "You're shameless."

"Hey, I did it for you, Ginger." He smoothed down her hair and deepened his voice. "You deserve only the best."

She lifted her face and received his kiss and for a few minutes they forgot about the bag. When they recovered themselves, Daniella sat on his lap and returned to the bag. She went through it, eager to see what else she could wear for him. "Well, it's obvious your favorite color is black."

"No, it's green," he said, lazily stroking the back of her neck.

"Then why didn't you get me anything in green?"

His hand paused. "Damn, I didn't think of that." He shrugged. "I just figured that black goes with everything."

"It's not like anyone's going to see it."

"I plan to."

"Besides you."

"So you're going to try them all on tonight, right?"

"I don't need to. I'm sure they'll fit."

"But just in case they don't we should try them on."

She sent him a significant look. "We?"

"Yes, you wear them and I'll…uh, supervise."

Daniella faked a pout. "I thought you liked me naked."

"I do. I'll help you in and out of each one."

They only made it through the first pair before getting lost in each other. Later Daniella did try each one and as promised he helped her in and out of them, which lasted all night.

Chapter 11

She knew that woman would be trouble. Vera looked at her daughter as Emma cleared away the dinner dishes. She hadn't thought Richard, no Trenton, that was his name now, would fall for the outsider. She believed the story he'd told her brother and knew he was still a good match for her daughter. She had a sense about these things. The outsider may have her hooks in him, but only for a time. Vera couldn't blame his choice. He was only a man and a man had certain needs, which Emma clearly wasn't going to meet. She'd brought her up to be more introverted. A good girl. Maybe too good. But a man needed more than a hot body. She slammed her hand against the table as she came up with a plan. "You may have lost him for a while, but you'll get him back."

Emma turned to her mother, confused. "What are you talking about?"

Vera hesitated. She hadn't told her daughter what she'd seen. Daniella was an indecent woman boldly answering the door in a man's robe. Showing off that she'd been in a man's place all night.

"I'm talking about Rich—Trenton."

"Is something wrong?"

"That woman is up at his place keeping his bed warm, but that's just for a little while. He can learn that a woman who can fill his belly is a lot more useful."

"Mom," Emma said, embarrassed. "Richard and I are just friends."

"His name is Trenton now and you can be more. He has to be. He's your last chance."

"There are other men."

"Where? Not in this town. The ones your age are either married or gone. You think I want you under my foot all the time?"

"No. I'll leave one day."

Vera continued as if Emma hadn't spoken. "That woman can't even cook."

"Her name is Daniella."

"I don't care what it is. He needs someone who will look after him. She's using him and he's too blind to see it."

"I like her."

Vera started to fill a container with biscuits. "You like anyone who pays attention to you. Is she the one who helped you paint up your face?"

"It's called makeup and yes she did. And if she makes Richard happy then let them be."

"She won't be around for long. And you can't miss your chance, you don't have many left at your age."

"I'm twenty—"

"Shh…you're too close to thirty to brag about your age anymore. You say it as if you're proud. I was married and a mother by the time I was in my early twenties. We're not going to let that woman rush in here and steal our dreams."

"Being with Rich—Trenton," Emma said to quickly correct herself when her mother gave her a stern look, "isn't my dream."

Again Vera ignored her. "I know she's young and pretty but age and beauty fade."

"I—"

"You're going to go there with this." She handed Emma two large containers.

Emma shook her head exasperated. "But, Mom, you just gave him food a couple days ago."

"Nothing's wrong with adding biscuits and home-made marmalade. Just say that I forgot to give it to him. He'll understand and think you're being considerate."

"Mom."

Vera held up a hand. "I got your father. I know how men think and I know how to catch one. Now no use arguing, I know what's best for you. Put some of that stuff on your face if you feel like it. I have to admit that it does add some color to you and you need whatever help you can get."

Emma took the containers, put on some makeup then got into her car just wanting to drive away. To drive away from her mother's expectations and her unfulfilled life. Drive away from the town that looked down on her. But she knew she had nowhere to go. So she'd do as her mother said, knowing that it wouldn't make a difference. She thought of Duane. She hadn't seen him in a while and wondered if she'd ever see him again.

He'd enjoy killing him. Duane watched Trenton and some woman from a distance playing with a dog. There Sheppard was, happy and laughing with his fiancée. Twice he'd come by but no one had been home, but the third time was the charm. Luck was on his side. He'd walked the distance not wanting to draw any attention by driving his car. He liked watching them undetected, it helped give him the courage to do what needed to be done. He'd no longer let Sheppard go on with his life as if he wasn't a murderer. He'd do his own justice. Duane reached for the gun tucked in his jeans.

"Hey, what are you doing out here?"

Duane spun around and saw Emma in her car with her windows rolled down. He quickly closed his jacket to hide the gun. "Just looking."

"I'm going to deliver some food to Richard, why don't you join me?"

He sent a nervous glance at the house then to her. "Uh…"

"Come on, it could give us a chance to talk."

"I'm really not in the mood to talk."

"Then you don't have to." She opened the passenger side. "I will."

Sheppard and his fiancée had disappeared. They'd probably gone inside. It was an opportunity to get close.

But he didn't want Emma to be involved. Then again it would get Sheppard off his game. Let him know that he was there and burst open his lies. Maybe he could tell his fiancée who she was really marrying. He got inside the car.

"I haven't seen you in a couple days. What have you been up to?"

"Nothing much," he said, glad that the drive up to the house was a short one. He followed Emma to the door and waited. He froze when Sheppard answered with a smile. "Emma, you and your mother have got to stop doing this."

Emma laughed. "If you can find a way to stop her from doing what she wants you need to tell me."

He looked past her and stared at him. The dog at his side growled. "Quiet, Layla," he said. "And who's your friend?"

"Duane."

He shook his hand without an ounce of recognition, fueling Duane's anger. "Nice to meet you," he said, opening the door wider. "Come in."

Duane stepped inside, gripping his hand into a fist. The bastard didn't even know him. His life meant so little to him that he didn't even recognize the face of the man whose life he'd destroyed. He felt his anger grow when a beautiful woman came into the room. Sheppard's fiancée. She gave him a bright smile and a warm hand-shake, reminding him of how long he'd been without the soft touch of a woman of his own. He'd be sorry to hurt her, but he would have to. In a way he'd be doing her a favor. "I'm Daniella," she said in greeting. "Emma, let me help you with that."

He couldn't let her leave the room. The dog was circling him in a menacing manner and he had to take control of the situation if his plan was to succeed. He grabbed her arm. "Sorry," he said, whipping out his gun and holding it to her head.

Daniella didn't scream, but Emma did. "Duane, what are you doing?"

Before he could reply, the dog sunk her teeth into his leg. He pointed the gun at the animal. "Get her off me or I'll kill her!"

Sheppard grabbed her collar and pulled her away. His gaze was steady as was his voice. "Now just relax. We can work this out."

Duane glared at him, tears of rage blurring his vision. He wanted to see fear in Sheppard's eyes, but cold brown eyes met him. "You don't remember me do you?"

"No."

"You watched my wife die. At first I was going to kill you, but this is even better. Now you're going to watch your love die. Everyone thinks you're a hero, but you're not. You're a coward and a fraud. You've fooled everyone here, but I know the truth."

Recognition finally dawned and Duane gained strength from the anguish that crossed the other man's face. He held out his hands, his gaze never leaving him, his voice neutral though his expression hadn't been. "Whatever happened in the past is between us, leave her out of it."

"I heard you're getting married."

He shook his head. "I'm not."

"Are you saying I'm a liar?"

"No, I'm saying your information is wrong."

"This year would have been my fifth wedding anniversary."

"Duane, I'm sorry," he said, sounding helpless, "but there's nothing I can do for you."

"You can rot in hell, you son of a bitch. I've tried to get over what you did. I've done the therapy, the travel and nothing's worked! The only thing that will work is an eye for an eye."

"You don't believe that."

He pressed the gun harder against Daniella's head. "You think I couldn't do it?"

"You're not that kind of man. And you wouldn't want to go to prison."

Duane's voice cracked. "You think my life isn't already a prison? If I can just see the agony on your face as you hold the one you love and see her life slipping away then it will be all worth it. That's all I want. To see you suffer. To see your anguish and helplessness."

"It won't last," Emma said.

Duane briefly shut his eyes, he'd forgotten she was there and he didn't want her kind, quiet voice to get to him. "It doesn't matter."

"A drunk driver killed my father and I wanted him to pay. I let it eat me up and later learned that the driver died a few years later and I felt hollow. I thought I would feel better, feel triumphant, but I didn't feel anything because his death didn't bring my father back and he wasn't sorry. Even if he was it didn't change what happened. Your wife wouldn't have wanted you to waste her love by hating. She'd want you to shine a light on the life she led. Let her life, no matter how short, be her legacy, not this."

Duane shoved Daniella away, wishing he could do the same to his despair. "I just want the pain to stop." He turned the gun on himself.

"It will," Emma said, her voice still quiet, but like a soothing balm to him. "I promise you it will, but you have to stop wishing things were different than they are."

"There's nothing worth living for."

"She loved you. Let her love for you live on. She wouldn't have wanted this for you. She would want you to enjoy all the things she can't give you. Live, love and grow old. Honor her memory."

Duane dropped the gun and crumbled to the ground. Trenton rushed to grab it while Emma knelt and hugged him. "Life is worth living."

He looked up at Trenton Sheppard for the first time, seeing just a man not his enemy, and he saw that he wasn't a man without feeling. He wasn't the monster he'd created in his mind. "Are you going to call the cops?"

Trenton pocketed the bullets he'd removed from the gun. "How did you find me?"

"It doesn't matter now."

"He didn't kill your wife," Daniella said.

Duane turned to her. "What?"

"Daniella, not now."

"No, he needs to know. It was all a setup. Someone else was responsible for the crash."

"But he was the one flying the plane. They said it was gross human error."

"There was something mechanically wrong with the plane. We have a strong trail and we're going to reveal the truth."

Trenton folded his arms. "How did you find me?" he repeated.

"Dr. Brooks called me. I'd met him during the trial and he's been keeping track of me. I thought he was a friend. He told me you were getting married on the day of Latisha's death."

Trenton pointed to a chair. "Sit down. Layla got you pretty good."

Duane glanced down at the blood dripping from his leg.

"I deserved it."

"I agree." Trenton disappeared a few seconds and returned with a first aid kit. He cleaned the wound. "It's deep but you won't need stitches."

"Why are you helping me?"

"It's what I do." He bandaged Duane up then gave him instructions on how to care for the bite.

Duane sighed and leaned his head back. "I never knew how tiring it is to hate somebody."

"I think we should go," Emma said.

Duane shook his head. "No, I'll face my punishment."

"I'm not calling the police," Trenton said.

He sent him a long look. "You should."

"But I'm not going to."

"Thanks."

Minutes later, Emma and Duane sat silently in her car as she drove him down Trenton's long driveway.

"Where can I drop you off?" Emma asked turning on to the main road.

"The nearest bridge."

She turned to him, alarmed. "Duane—"

"No, I just like looking at the water flowing past. It calms me."

"Oh."

"You must think I'm crazy."

"No."

"Why did you stop me?"

She took his hand. "Because your life is precious to me."

"A stranger?"

"You're not anymore. You're my friend."

He released a sour laugh. "You must not have many."

"No, I don't. You're my third one."

Emma's unbridled care and warmth washed over him. He wanted to live and not be so bitter. He looked down at her hand—his lifeline—and took hold.

"I'm sorry about everything," he said, valiantly blinking back tears.

"I understand."

The fact that she was nonjudgmental made him relax. He believed that she did understand him and that made all the difference. Just as she'd been good to him, he'd be good to her. And for the first time as he let Latisha go, he realized he wanted to love again. "Have you ever been to Niagara Falls?"

"No, I haven't been anywhere."

"You'd like it there. Such beauty and strength. Latisha and I…" He stopped.

"Go on. Tell me about her."

And he did and as he spoke, he let himself finally release her for good.

Trenton stared out the window until Emma's car was out of sight then he took the bullets out of his pocket and cradled them in his hand. He couldn't ignore what he'd suspected many years ago about his old friend. Brooks had tried to kill Daniella and now him. He had to uncover what he wanted to protect. "Duane's right. I have you fooled. I'm not a hero."

Daniella walked over to the window and stood beside him. "Yes, you are."

He laughed bitterly and tossed the bullets up in the air then gripped them in his fist. "That's what my wife thought at first. She liked what I did. How it sounded. What it looked like to the public. Then when that image faded she had no use for me. I did everything I could to revive Latisha but I couldn't. I failed." He shoved the bullets back into his pocket. "Everybody loves a hero, but nobody loves an ordinary man." He turned from the window and sat on the couch, feeling as if he were bearing the weight of the world.

"I do."

He shook his head and flashed a sad smile. "No, you have some idealized version of me in your head. You've only seen me succeed. You've never seen me not get to a person in time or fail to resuscitate someone."

"I don't need to see that. I know you're just an ordinary man. I know you listen to country music, walk around your house in the nude—"

A quick grin touched the corner of his mouth. "Only when you're there to watch."

"You don't cook, you send postcards to your parents even though you haven't seen them in years and know that they would like to at least get a letter or email or phone call. You're arrogant, impatient and have a morbid sense of humor. And these are your finer qualities. That sounds pretty ordinary to me."

"And you like this ordinary man?"

Daniella saddled him. "I like him a lot."

He wrapped his arms around her waist. "Because he's such a good lover?"

Daniella pushed her hand through his hair. "Did I mention you're conceited, too?"

"Just file it under arrogant." He bit his lip and searched her face. "So why?"

"Why what?"

"Why do you like this ordinary man so much?" He shook his head. "Let's not fool ourselves. If I hadn't saved your life you wouldn't be here."

"No, I'd be dead."

"So it's all a sense of gratitude."

"It's more than that. I think I fell in love with you the moment your father told me about your first pet."

"Fell in love?" he said, his voice unsteady.

"Yes," she said firmly. "I fell in love with you as I

listened to him talk about how and why you became a medic. I knew that you were the kind of man who could steal my heart and I decided I'd let you do so. But I can see that I have an advantage because I know a lot about you and you know little about me."

He tightened his hold. "So tell me about yourself."

"I'm the youngest of four daughters. Usually just the tagalong. No one had ever considered me a leader until I met you. You believed in me and trusted me. You saw something in me no one ever has. You made me feel useful and needed. I loved you for that the most."

His mouth curved into a devastating grin.

She felt herself smiling back, feeling a glow of happiness fill her. "What?"

"I'm glad I didn't take the train."

She loved him. He was still too wary to believe it. Fayola had promised to love him in front of six hundred people and that hadn't lasted. He sat in the vet's office barely listening; he'd stopped when he learned the diagnosis was exactly what Dr. Khan had told him.

Layla's tumor was located close to the pituitary gland, near to the brain. Poor Layla, her age was against her with the recovery rate for dogs her age with a brain tumor rather low. But Trenton knew there was only one choice: to go ahead with the surgery. The decision was made to remove the tumor and proceed with radiation therapy, based on the pathology result and chemotherapy, if needed. Trenton hoped that Layla would not have to undergo all three treatment options, and for the first time in a long time, he whispered a silent prayer. He couldn't lose Layla, not now. He absently thanked the doctor and headed for the truck while Daniella stayed behind to ask a few more questions. Minutes later she joined him, smiling.

"Why are you smiling? Nothing has changed. Layla still needs an expensive surgery I can't afford."

"I have good news for you. I've scheduled the surgery and you don't have to pay a cent."

"Are you serious? How did you manage that?"

"I worked my charm and I told him that you're a volunteer EMT and Layla helps you. He has a special foundation he set up to help working dogs like Layla."

"But she isn't—"

"She helps you and you help others. Just accept it."

He could feel himself breathing again. Layla would get the surgery. She had a chance to live.

"I can't thank you enough. I'm taking you out to dinner." The next day he took Daniella to a stylish restaurant then they went to the park and sat on a bench, watching the children play. One little boy about three ran up to Trenton and gave him his ball.

Trenton shook his head. "No, it's yours."

The boy continued to hold the ball out. Trenton took it then tossed it to him. "Nice job." The boy giggled and started to talk in a childish gibberish Daniella couldn't understand, but Trenton nodded his head as if he could.

His mother rushed up to them. "Thank goodness. I lost sight of him. He just started running to you."

"I know they can move fast. That's okay, we were having fun."

She picked up the boy and Trenton waved. "Bye, Gordon, and stay close to your mother."

Daniella turned to him, shocked. "How did you know his name was Gordon?"

"He told us. He also told me about his goldfish and his best friend and his favorite ball."

"I could hardly understand him."

He shrugged. "It's nothing. I have a niece and nephew."

"So do I but I still couldn't understand that little boy."

"It's a gift," he said with a smirk then he took her hand. "Come on, let's walk."

But children kept crossing their path. Next a little girl lost her balloon and began to cry, Trenton picked up a flower nearby and with her parents' permission gave it to her. He whispered something and in seconds she was all smiles again. Another child asked him to play with him and started to follow him until her parents grabbed her.

"You have a magical way with children. It was the same after the crash when Anna and Mark stayed close to you."

"I don't know why."

Daniella wrapped her arm through his. "I do. You're the son of Father Christmas."

He laughed.

"Remember I met them. I know your secret."

He winked. "And you'll keep it for me."

"Of course," she said. "As long as you never let him know how naughty I've been."

Trenton laughed again, kissing her affectionately on

the cheek. "Don't worry, there are certain things he'll never know."

This time Daniella laughed, noticing how young and vibrant he looked once again. It wasn't just the glow of her love for him that had changed him. He'd changed and she knew he was letting himself enjoy life again. Being with him and seeing his joy made her life just that much sweeter, too.

Their moods weren't as buoyant on the morning of Layla's surgery. Daniella went with Trenton to the veterinary hospital. Both were tearful when Layla was given a sedative and handed over to the surgical nurse, and then for the next two and a half hours they waited. The surgeon came out and told them that everything went okay. Luckily, the tumor had been contained and had not metastasized. Thankfully, three weeks later the lab result showed that the tumor was not cancerous. Trenton and Daniella celebrated by renting an old movie and eating popcorn through the night.

Over the next several weeks, Layla had to be kept quiet during her recovery period, which wasn't much of a problem. She was extremely weak. Due to the location of the tumor treatment, her nervous system had to be examined regularly by a CAT scan. The doctor had told Trenton that it was important to watch for any complications, one of which included problems with weakened swallowing reflexes that was sometimes caused as a result of increased pressure of cerebrospinal fluid in the skull cavity. But, in spite of all the physical therapy, Layla did not appear to want to recover too fast, she was enjoying all the attention she was getting.

Daniella spent time with Layla during the day while Trenton took over at night. Trenton bought her a printer to attach to her laptop and during the weeks she spent at Trenton's place she'd sold six stories, and told Sophia—and her sisters—she was all right. Daniella and Trenton also followed up on her investigation, searching for Brooks's connection with the airplane company.

Each day Trenton left early and returned home late, never willing to share how his day had been besides *fine*. Daniella didn't press him for more details and he was grateful for it. Trenton had made progress in his search for Daniella's abductors. He'd gotten to the first one, a chubby man with a fondness for expensive shoes, nicknamed "Roll," because he was reputed to like to "roll on" any fine female that crossed his path whether by force or otherwise.

When Trenton found him getting his shoes shined, he'd been cocky and sure of himself until Trenton had yanked one of his fine shoes off his foot and, using a pocket knife, began carving into the fine leather—destroying its smooth surface and tearing at its seams. He'd never heard a man squeal so loudly.

"All right! All right!" Roll cried. Trenton had taken him around the corner from the shoe-shine stand where they couldn't be seen. Roll stared at his shoe. "What do you want?"

"Where's L.Z.?"

Roll's eyes flew up, a new horror entering his face. "I didn't say L.Z. had anything to do with it."

"You don't have to, I know he did."

Roll held up his hands. "I have nothing to say against him."

Trenton gripped the second shoe between his hands and began to fold it. "I wonder how flexible this is."

Roll held out his hands. "Do you know how much that costs?"

Trenton narrowed his eyes. "Tell me what I want to hear and maybe I'll start to care."

"He's a killer, you know."

"I know. Where can I find him?"

Roll gave him three possible addresses and a phone number. "But you didn't hear this from me."

"No." He tossed the shoe on the ground.

Roll scrambled to get it then held it up as if it were a damaged work of art.

Trenton folded his arms and leaned against one of the buildings. "I heard you have a reputation."

Roll put on his shoe without interest. "Every man has a reputation."

"I heard you have a reputation with the ladies. Did you try to improve that reputation with her?"

Roll's head shot up. "Did she say anything?"

Trenton pushed himself from the wall. "Should she have?"

Roll took several steps back. "I didn't touch her. There wasn't time and I wasn't there for that."

"Never stopped you before."

"I've never been convicted."

"You know the ones to choose. The kind that don't talk."

Roll licked his lips. "Nothing happened. I swear."

"Good." Trenton lifted his hand to give him a pat on the shoulder, but stopped when Roll flinched. "You come near her again and I won't be this nice."

He wasn't nice at all when he caught up with L.Z. He met him outside a pool hall and didn't give him a chance to talk. He didn't care what the other man had to say… at first. After getting most of his aggression out on the skinny man's face, Trenton asked him some questions.

"Did Brooks hire you?"

L.Z. wiped the blood from his mouth and spit out a tooth. "How's my mother doing? Oh, that's right, you wouldn't know. You haven't been home."

"How much did he give you?"

"Don't know what you're talking about. You must have me confused with someone else."

"She'll recognize your voice," Trenton said.

"She'll be too terrified to testify."

Yes, Trenton remembered her fear and how close to death she'd been. He knew he couldn't kill him as much as he wanted to because right now he wasn't going to give him the information he wanted. He'd have to try another way. A harder way. L.Z. wasn't a healthy man and he was skinny for a reason. He'd spent most of his food money on his habit. Trenton guessed from L.Z.'s lucidity and confidence that he'd recently scored a hit and would be in need of another soon. He was going to make sure that L.Z. didn't get it.

"You're right," Trenton agreed. "There's no need to discuss this."

"Glad you're starting to see things my way." L.Z. turned and seconds later he was seeing stars. Trenton bound his hands and feet just as he had done to Daniella then he drove him to a rundown motel and waited. It didn't take long for the withdrawal symptoms to hit. The shakes, the headaches, the nausea. Soon L.Z. was pleading with him for relief. Trenton watched him writhe on the floor in agony. "Tell me what I want to know."

L.Z. told him everything. Once he was satisfied, Trenton put him in the trunk, drove him to his dealer and dropped him off, without removing the duct tape. A couple of days later, it was reported that an unidentified man had been found dead in a parking lot, fitting L.Z.'s description. It was a suspected overdose. Trenton guessed that L.Z.'s heart, which had never been strong, hadn't been able to take the stress he'd been under. He felt for L.Z.'s mother, but felt nothing else.

Over the weeks he'd had no trouble explaining his long days of absence, sometimes disappearing for two or three days at a time. But he had a much harder time explaining away his bruises and scars, saying they were work related.

"But what happened?" Daniella said, concerned by the bruising on his knuckles, as she rewrapped one of his hands.

"Just a work accident," he said, trying not to wince.

"What were you doing?"

Trenton briefly saw himself pummeling L.Z.'s face. "Removing some garbage," he said, then kissed her and took her attention off his wounds. He was glad now that she was safe. Next, he planned how he would deal with Brooks. He was glad to be able to focus on Layla's healing and being with Daniella for several days. Caring for Layla had brought the two of them closer together.

They fed Layla, bathed her, massaged her and, as part of her recovery, hired an acupuncturist who would come in on a daily basis to give her treatments. Trenton indulged her further, by buying her a bag full of gourmet dog treats and several squeaky dog toys, her favorites.

Although she had a large collection of toys, she was like a puppy whenever Trenton brought her a new toy to add to her trophies. As she recovered, Layla's uncoordinated movements and "drunken" gait started to improve, and she didn't recognize or know that one lasting outcome of the tumor was that she was left with a visible limp and diminished vision in her right eye. But none of this curtailed her desire to enjoy life. As Layla continued to heal, Daniella continued to search.

"Pascal, I want you to look into a company called Sheldon Industries."

"What am I looking for?"

"I'm not sure. Complaints, anything. Trenton said something was wrong with the plane and I believe him."

"Okay, I'll see what I can come up with."

A week later Pascal called. "Your hunch was right. Sheldon Industries was bought by a huge investment company three years ago. But that's not the real issue. I looked into Dr. Brooks. His practice had a major turnaround about the same time of the court case decision. There's definitely a link. My source also spoke to a former employee who was fired because he'd complained about possible safety regulations."

"Great. Send me what you've found."

"I will. This is a cover-up, Dani. This is fantastic material. You've hit on a perfect story."

"I told you I don't care about the story, I just want to clear Trenton's name."

"When you read what I'm sending you you'll change your mind."

He was partially right. As she read what Pascal's investigator had sent him, the picture became clearer. Sheldon Industries was struggling and was in the process of negotiating a merger when the crash happened. Not wanting the other company to back out of the deal, they hired Dr. Brooks to forge the lab work and blame the crash on the pilot, Trenton. With him out of the way no one would look deeper and their secret was safe. Daniella relayed this to Trenton while they were at dinner that evening.

"I thought so, but we have no proof. It's all speculative."

"We have bank records."

"You have a disgruntled employee, not tied to Sheldon and Brooks. It's all in your head."

"I know I'm right."

"I think so, too, but we've got to get proof."

Daniella glanced down when her phone rang then looked at Trenton. "It's your father."

Chapter 12

"Go on and answer it," Trenton said.

"Do you want to talk to him?"

He shook his head. "No. I can't."

"Why not?"

"I just can't." He left the room.

Daniella sighed then answered. "Hi, Mr. Sheppard."

"Are you okay? I hadn't heard from you in a few days and you'd told us you'd let us know how things went."

"I'm fine. I'm sorry I didn't get back to you." She didn't want to worry them so she decided not to mention the kidnapping. "I spoke to Dr. Brooks and his nurse and I am following up a great lead. It's possible there was a major cover-up and Trenton was just an unfortunate victim." She told Mr. Sheppard her suspicions.

"Great. I know people so if you let me see the lab work…"

"I will. I have a few more things to do first then I'll get back to you. Together we'll clear Trenton's name."

"Bye."

Daniella hung up the phone and took down some notes.

Trenton returned and stood in the entryway. "You must think I'm a coward," he said.

She laughed. "You're the least cowardly person I know, but I think you're wrong not to talk to him."

"I just want to be cleared first. I want to be able to stand tall."

"You can stand tall now. They believe in you."

"They want to believe in me, but I have to prove…"

She took his hand, her voice tender. "You don't have to prove anything. They love you just the way you are."

His gaze fell. "I need time to…"

"One thing I've learned is that no one is promised tomorrow. What if this is your last chance to speak to your father. Would you want it to end like this?"

"He'll ask me questions I can't answer."

"So?"

"The one thing I never wanted to do was disappoint him and I know that I have."

Daniella shrugged. "So face it. It won't go away." She held up the phone. "Call him back."

He rubbed his chin. "I'm going to make my mother cry."

"Probably."

He sighed then took the phone. "What do I say?"

"Just start with hello."

Trenton dialed then waited. "They're not home," he said and started to disconnect.

Daniella snatched the phone from him. "It's only rung twice. Give them time." She waited with her heart pounding. Perhaps they weren't home. She didn't want them to miss this opportunity.

"Hello?" a deep, familiar voice said.

Her heart soared. "Hello, Mr. Sheppard. It's Daniella again. Um…someone wants to talk to you."

Trenton shook his head and held up his hands. "I've changed my mind."

"Hold on one moment." She pressed the phone against her chest. "You will speak to him now or I will never sleep with you again."

He grinned. "Yes, you will."

"Want to try me?"

His grin fell. "You're serious?"

"Yes."

"You call that a threat?"

"Yes, now stop stalling and make your choice."

She held out the phone.

Trenton flexed his hand then grabbed it. He held it up to his ear and closed his eyes. "Hello, Dad. Dad? Uh… yes I can wait." Trenton sank into a chair and looked up at Daniella. "He went to get my mother."

"Good. I'll leave you."

He grabbed her wrist. "No, don't. Please."

She sat down beside him.

"Yes, I'm still here. Uh-huh. I'm fine. I'm going to put you on speaker."

"Can we come see you?"

"Not yet, but I hope to visit you soon." He waited for the disappointment, the pain, the scolding but he just heard silence. "Dad?"

"The grill's waiting when you're ready to come home."

"Where do you think you're going?" Vera demanded as Emma packed her things.

"I'm leaving."

"To go where?"

"Niagara Falls."

"You can't just leave me here."

"You've wanted me gone a long time and I'm making that wish come true."

"Running off with some man. You're going to regret it."

"I've been scared all my life. I'm not going to be scared anymore. I'm going to travel and meet people and help them." She closed her suitcase, picked up two other bags and marched outside where an expensive-looking car sat in the driveway. Vera saw a man get out and take the suitcase from her daughter and place it in the trunk. Vera recognized him from the diner, but there was something different about him. He didn't have the same melancholy air that had been over him like a dark cloud. He was a rather good-looking man, something she hadn't noticed before. What would he want with her daughter?

"You're going off with him?" Vera asked, although she already knew the answer.

"Yes."

"You're still plain. He'll have his way with you then toss you to the side when he finds someone better."

"That's where you're wrong, Mrs. Clegg," Duane said, slamming the trunk closed. "I plan to marry her."

Vera stared at him for a long moment, not sure she'd heard him right. "Marry her?"

"Yes."

"What for?" she scoffed. "She doesn't have any money."

"She's a gem. She's all the riches I need. Besides I don't need money. I have enough so that I don't have to work if I don't want to. She won't either. I'm going to take her to all the places I've been and more. I'm going to care for her and love her in a way you never could."

Vera looked at him speechless. Emma was in just as much shock as her mother when she looked at him. "You want to marry me?"

Duane cupped her face in his hands and held it gently. "I will marry you and I will make you happy," he said and then he kissed her. Not a quick kiss, but a deep, loving one. It was Emma's first kiss, so initially she held her mouth closed, but slowly and expertly Duane persuaded her lips open and sent her mind spinning. When he drew away he left her mouth burning for more.

Vera glared at the pair, jealous of their newfound love, but unwilling to admit it. She'd never thought that Emma would leave the town—or leave her. She watched the pair get into the car already looking like newlyweds, and for the first time she realized how much she'd taken her daughter for granted. How she'd always berated her, scolded her. How unkind she had been. She ran up to the car and tapped on the window.

"If you give me any grandbabies, you'll let me know, right? Maybe I can come and visit."

Emma smiled and for the first time Vera saw how beautiful her daughter was and how Duane's love made her glow. "Yes, Mom, you'll always be welcome."

At last she had the final puzzle piece. The lab work was as the nurse suspected. It wasn't Trenton's blood. It couldn't have been. She went to tell Trenton, who sat watching TV. Suddenly his image appeared on the screen with the words *A Hero Wronged?* "We have Pulitzer prize winning author Pascal Bordeaux who is out to right a wrong," the anchorwoman said.

Daniella stood paralyzed, unable to process what she was seeing. All the things she'd shared with Pascal he was claiming as his own. Everything she'd sent to him—pictures, notes—he'd used to create his own story. She'd wanted to give Trenton the time to tell his own story if he wanted to, not spread out his life for all to see. There was Pascal discussing the case and all the details. How had it gotten this far? How would Trenton ever trust her again? What would his parents think? They'd all think she used them.

Trenton turned to her, stunned. "Did you know about this?"

"No, I swear. I gave him some notes, but that's all."

"Is this the Pascal you told me about? The one who convinced you to find me?"

"Yes, he helped me."

"You gave him pictures from my life, my childhood, and shared intimate details?"

"Just in the beginning when I just saw you as a story, but I stopped and told him I wasn't going to write about you. I just used his contacts to find out more about Sheldon Industries. I thought he was helping."

"Now everyone in town is going to know what you've been up to. And without an arrest Brooks is going to come after you again. But I'm going to get to him first. You're going to go home. Pascal has also made himself a target, but he's too visible to wipe out, but I bet you he can be bought."

"You don't believe me."

"It doesn't matter what I believe right now."

"I…this wasn't supposed to happen."

Trenton stood. "Get your things together. We don't have time."

There was no goodbye, no farewell. Trenton saw her to her car then turned and went inside, closing the door. She knew he'd do what he needed to do to protect her but Pascal had torn them apart. She had been naive. And now she had lost him.

Chapter 13

Daniella looked inside the overcrowded classroom at the college while Pascal stood in front at the podium and held them captive. She opened the door. "Listen up, class, you're about to learn a lesson on ethics."

"Daniella, not now."

"Why not? You taught me a lesson and I want to share it with everyone. They deserve to know what the real world is like."

"You're making a fool of yourself, Daniella."

"Just tell me why."

"Why what?"

"Why did you steal my story?"

"I didn't steal anything. You wouldn't have had a story if it hadn't been for me. You asked for my help every step of the way. It was *our* story. I gave you feedback, contacts—"

"While I did all the work."

"I admit that I should have put your name on the by-line. I will next time in the follow-up article."

"There won't be a next time."

"I knew that you were too soft. That you'd let all this great material go to waste just because you have feelings for him. But this isn't just one man's story. It's every man's story. It's our right as the public to know what goes on behind the scenes. What corruptions are out there. Because of me, the officials are looking into both Brooks and Sheldon Industries. Trenton will be vindicated."

"Because of you?" Daniella's voice cracked in disbelief.

"Dani," he said with a hint of regret. "I said this story was out of your league and I proved I was right."

"You plagiarized—"

"I didn't plagiarize. I didn't steal your words."

"You took my notes and—"

"I wrote my own story from the facts you gathered. The facts don't belong to you. That's how it's done. No one owns a story or its premise."

"You're a bigger jerk than I thought."

"No, not a jerk." A smug, triumphant grin spread across his face. "Just a writer."

"No, a parasite who needs a host in order to survive."

"The fact is I do survive and there's nothing you can do about it."

"You're a fraud, Parry Baines, and one day someone will prove it." Daniella stormed out of the classroom with the same passion in which she'd entered, leaving the crowded classroom in stunned silence.

He'd have to get out of the country. Brooks hurriedly gathered the papers he'd kept in a safety deposit box hidden in his bedroom. The authorities couldn't reach him in Spain or Portugal and better yet, the men he'd taken over a quarter of a million dollars from to make sure that Trenton took all the blame for the crash wouldn't know how to find him. He jumped when a scream pierced the silence of his large house. Brooks raced down the hall and saw his wife paralyzed in the middle of the room with her eyes wide. When he turned his gaze he noticed the other figure in the room—the cause for her fear—Trenton.

Brooks covered his own growing fear with anger. "How the hell did you get in here?"

Trenton shook his head. "Try another question." He went over to a couch and casually took a seat.

"What do you want?"

His mouth spread into a thin smile. "That's better."

"Listen I—"

"Sit down."

Brooks paused. "What?"

Trenton pointed to the seat opposite him. Brooks glanced at his wife then took the seat and motioned for her to do the same. Once she was also seated he said, "I don't know why you're here, but I'm sure we can come to an understanding."

"I doubt it."

Brooks swallowed and licked his lips. He knew that

Trenton could be a hard man to manipulate. He had to tread carefully. "What can I do for you?"

"You were my father's protégé. My father trusted you and so did I. I won't make that mistake this time."

"I told you that there was nothing I could do. I only did my job."

"I thought the doctor's oath was 'First do no harm.' I know about your connection with Sheldon Industries and I know what you've been up to the last several weeks."

Brooks felt beads of sweat on his forehead, but kept his voice level. "I haven't been up to anything."

"Daniella Duvall. Does her name ring a bell?"

He shrugged. "She came to ask me a few questions."

Trenton rested his arm on the back of the couch, appearing to look casual though Brooks knew he wasn't. "Yes, and you tried to kill her."

"I don't know what you're talking about."

"Then I'll remind you. I had a chance to chat with two men you hired to kidnap and scare Daniella." He stared down at his hand and flexed it into a fist. "They were really reluctant to talk to me at first, but once they stopped screaming, I got them to tell me everything." His eyes met Brooks.

Brooks held his gaze. "If you tortured them I'm sure they said whatever you wanted them to say. You can't prove anything. Besides, drug addicts make unreliable witnesses."

"How did you know they were drug addicts?"

Brooks hesitated, recognizing his slip. "Those types usually are."

Trenton slowly nodded as if considering his words. "Fine, let's pretend the kidnapping had nothing to do with you. What about poor Duane Martin? Do you deny you sent him after me? He told me you led him to me."

"He's a disturbed man. He's been in and out of grief counseling and is unable to handle his emotions. You can't trust what he says."

Trenton shifted his gaze to Fayola, who sat still by Brooks's side. "What was more tempting—the money or my wife?"

"I—"

Trenton held up his hand. "Never mind. Everything that comes out of your mouth is a lie. I know what you did. I even think I know why you did it."

"Then what do you want? Money?"

Trenton lowered his gaze. "You're smarter than that, Brooks."

"What do you want? Just tell me what you want."

Trenton kept his gaze lowered and remained silent. As the seconds stretched on Brooks lost his patience. He jumped up and shouted. "What the hell do you want me to do? I can't change the past."

"Actually I don't want anything from you." Trenton turned his gaze to Fayola. She was still beautiful and wore her hair down in elaborate microbraids. As he stared at her he allowed himself to remember the hopes and dreams they'd made for the future together. "I wanted Fayola to see the choice she made."

"She doesn't know anything."

"You never wanted to know."

Her eyes filled with tears. "Trenton, I'm sorry."

"Me, too."

He stood when there was a knock on the door. "That will be the police."

Brooks's eyes widened. "What?"

"The police have a few questions to ask you about the two drug addicts you don't know anything about." He opened the door and welcomed the officers in.

"I'll fight this," Brooks said to Trenton after the officers read him his rights.

"Try. I'm going to win this time."

Trenton watched them lead him away. "You should probably follow your husband to the precinct."

Fayola touched his arm and for a moment Trenton allowed himself to dream. This was the moment he'd always wanted. That she'd beg for his forgiveness and want him back. "I didn't know anything, I swear. I'm just as horrified as you are. I was so wrong."

"Forget it." He took a deep breath. "Just tell me one thing. Why him?"

"It wasn't something we planned, it just happened."

"Before or after the trial?"

Fayola wiped away her tears. "I was always true to you. I loved you."

"Just not enough," he said, unaffected by her tears.

"We could start over."

Trenton briefly shut his eyes, ready to feel victorious but feeling empty instead. She wanted him back. She still had feelings for him, but the difference was he didn't have feelings for her. He felt no pain. He was finally free. He moved away.

"No point, Fay. There's nothing to start over with," he said then walked out of her life forever.

At home Trenton tried to call Daniella but her phone went immediately to voice mail. Why wouldn't she clear her messages or at least pick up? He looked down at Layla. "I'm sure she's all right." Maybe she'd disappeared and didn't want anything to do with him. Maybe it had all been an act. Perhaps she and Pascal had been in it together the whole time. Fine, he'd move on without her. Layla dropped a toy at his feet. He tossed it to her and it rolled under the couch. "Sorry girl, that wasn't fair. I'll get it." He looked under the couch and saw a folded piece of paper. He pulled the paper out and unfolded it. It was a pawn slip for an antique ring and earrings—eight thousand dollars. He looked at Layla. That was how much her surgery had cost. *You don't have to pay a cent,* he remembered her saying, because she'd paid it for him. No one who could do this would betray him. She was genuine and he needed to find her.

Chapter 14

It was a cool summer day when Marnie Sheppard's dream finally came true. She was removing weeds from her garden when she looked up and saw a man with a golden lab coming up the path. He'd walked that path before—rushing up it when he'd come home from his first day at school, after he'd led his track team to a state victory, when he'd wanted to introduce her to his fiancée. He hadn't walked that path in a long time. But there he was. He stopped when he noticed her staring at him.

"Hi, Mom."

She scrambled to her feet and ran to him, throwing her arms around him once he was within reach. She squeezed him tight and tears sprang to her eyes.

"Mom, I can't breathe."

She reluctantly loosened her hold and gazed up at

him. "I just want to make sure you're real." She touched his face in awe. "Is my baby really home?"

"Yes, for a while anyway."

"You're leaving again," she said, suddenly anxious.

"No, just…" He shook his head. "There's something I have to do. It's a long story."

"I don't care. I want to hear everything." She looped her arm through his. "Come inside and get something to eat."

"Where's Dad?"

"Running one of his errands, he'll be home soon and he'll be so happy to see you."

Marnie wouldn't leave his side. After requesting snacks from the housekeeper she sat beside him and touched his sleeve and held his hand and just gazed at him.

Trenton took her hand in his. "I'm sorry for all the pain I put you through."

"No," she said, too quickly. "I—"

He shook his head. "Mom, please let me apologize. I shouldn't have made you worry for all those years."

"We're going to make up those years."

"Yes."

She turned when she heard a car drive up. "That will be your father."

Trenton stood suddenly, looking awkward. "What should I do?"

"I don't know." She paused. "I know." She shoved him toward the door. "Go and open it."

"Open the door?"

"Yes," she said, giving him another hard shove. "Don't argue with me."

Trenton sighed then swung the door open just as his father was putting the key in the lock. Gilford stared at him, obviously stunned, then slowly crumbled to the ground.

Trenton rushed toward him. "Dad!"

He covered his face and shook his head. "I can't believe it." He stared up at him with tears swimming in his eyes. "Is it really you?"

"Yes," Trenton said in a choked voice.

Gilford held out his hand. "Help me up."

Trenton took his hand and helped him to his feet and then his father pulled him close and gave him a bear hug. "It's been too long," he said, patting him on the back.

Trenton could only nod.

Gilford rested his arm on Trenton's shoulders and the two men walked into the house. "Our boy's come home, Marnie." He lifted his voice. "Bonita, you can stop hiding, come out and say hello."

At first there was silence then the housekeeper cautiously came around the corner with her head bowed.

Trenton sniffed the air. "Something smells good. Did you cook something special because you knew I was coming?"

She shook her head, keeping her gaze lowered. "Don't be kind to me, I don't deserve it. Not yet."

Trenton rested his hand on her shoulder. "It's all in the past."

Her voice wavered. "Did they tell you all that I did?"

"Doesn't matter."

"And my son—"

"Won't hurt anyone again."

She glanced up in surprise, then a cruel smile spread on her face. "Good."

Trenton opened his arms. "Do I get a hug now?"

Bonita shyly hugged him.

Trenton turned his cheek to her. "How about a kiss?"

She laughed and playfully slapped him. "You're still a bad boy."

Marnie clasped her hands together. "And we have to convince him not to leave us again."

Gilford looked at him with concern. "Is that true?"

"I have to find someone."

Gilford tilted his head. "Is it that beautiful woman who first set out to find you?"

"Daniella? Yes."

"How did you manage to lose her?"

"Gilford, be fair," Marnie said. "Who says he lost her?"

"A man doesn't have to chase down a woman he owns."

Marnie shook her head. "You don't own a woman."

Gilford smiled. "I'll convince you later."

She blushed. "Gilford. Really."

He returned his attention to his son. "So what happened?"

"We had a misunderstanding," Trenton said.

"She's the one for you."

Trenton patted the top of Layla's head. "I know that now."

"I hate to see you go so soon, but I understand she's a woman worth keeping."

"I think so."

"Before you go, we have to do one thing first."

Marnie frowned. "What?"

The Sheppard men shared a smile then said in unison, "Fire up the grill!"

Sophia Carlton wasn't in the mood for visitors, especially the one that showed up on her doorstep. The one who had caused her best friend to lose all sense and go after a crazy story, to unravel a mystery, then break her heart. She opened the door then rested her hip against the frame, making it clear she would not welcome him inside. "Yes?"

"I'm looking for Daniella."

"She's not here."

"Could you tell me where she is?"

"Maybe."

Trenton held out his hand. "My name is Trenton Sheppard and I—"

Sophia folded her arms. Trenton was better looking than his pictures, but that didn't matter now. "I know who you are."

"I just want to talk to her."

"Why should I let you see her? You're the reason she's been in bed for days."

"Maybe Layla can cheer her up," he said, tugging on the leash in his hand. His face eased into a smile. "They're good friends."

For the first time Sophia noticed the dog sitting quietly at his side. She was surprised by how infectious Trenton's smile was. It lit up his face and made her want to smile, too. She hadn't expected the smile, she'd expected him to get annoyed or surly with her, but instead he seemed not only patient and understanding, but determined. Sophia sighed, knowing that she wouldn't easily get rid of this big man, and not knowing if she wanted to. She could see why her friend had fallen for him. "It was all a mistake. Daniella thought Pascal was helping her."

"I know." He waited.

Sophia let her arms fall, she didn't have to let him in, but she knew he wasn't going to leave. "She's at her sister's place."

"Which one? She has three."

"She's with Izzy." Sophia lifted a warning brow. "Alex is there, too."

"Alex?"

Sophia nodded. "Yes, my older brother. We're a close family so you'd better watch yourself."

A teasing gleam entered Trenton's eyes. "I'll keep that in mind."

Sophia smiled, glad that he'd taken her threat in fun. Yes, she liked him and felt she was doing the right thing by sending him to Daniella. "Good, then I'll give you the address."

Across town, Alex Carlton stood beside his wife and shook his head in concern. "How long has she been like this?" he asked Isabella as they both watched Daniella sitting listlessly in the conservatory. Isabella had invited her over when Sophia had complained that Daniella wouldn't get out of bed. Now she was up but the summer sun ceased to raise her spirits. Their two daughters were napping upstairs.

"She won't talk, won't play with Kati, won't eat. I don't know what to do."

"Give her time."

"I'm hoping Gabby and Mariella can help me."

His eyes widened. "Mariella's coming? Why didn't you warn me?"

She shot her husband a glance. "Stop overreacting. Tony is stopping by, too, so you won't be lonely."

The doorbell rang. He checked the window and saw the car. "Good, it's Gabby."

"Mariella isn't that bad."

"People say the same thing about vinegar."

"Come on," she said leading him to the foyer where the housekeeper greeted Gabby and Tony.

"Where are the kids?" Alex asked.

"With the babysitter," Tony said. "I didn't think Daniella would be in the mood for them."

"You're right," Isabella said.

The two men disappeared upstairs while Isabella led Gabby to the conservatory.

"Dani, you have a visitor."

Daniella tried to smile. "Hi."

"I bought you some pasta salad for later today."

"Thanks."

Moments later they heard the doorbell and then Mariella's voice. Isabella rushed out to meet her. "Dani is very fragile. Be tactful," she said in a low voice.

"I'm always tactful," she said, tossing Isabella her scarf as if she were the housekeeper instead of mistress of the house. "Where is she?"

Isabella put Mariella's scarf away. "In the conservatory."

She strolled into the room and took a seat. "You need time away. Tell me where you want to go and I'll make it happen."

"No, thanks," Daniella said.

"You should talk to him," Isabella said. "You shouldn't ignore his calls."

"I don't know what to say."

"You don't have to always know what to say. Listen to what he has to say."

"It will be too painful. Nothing I say will matter anyway. I know what he thinks of me. Everyone he's trusted has betrayed him and he'll think I'm the same."

"You don't know that."

"I do. I know him."

"And he should know you. Daniella, you're miserable. At least apologize."

"I wish I'd never gone after him."

"I'm glad you did. You learned a lot about yourself and Pascal."

Daniella gripped her fist. "I wish I'd punched him. But I blame myself. I shouldn't have trusted him. I've hurt so many people. I thought I was doing something good. But I've failed."

"Have a fun rebound romance and get over him," Mariella said.

Isabella pinched her.

"Or call him," she corrected, rubbing her arm.

"He might get back with his ex-wife now that she knows he was innocent and her husband had helped set him up."

"If he takes her back then he deserves her."

"No, he deserves only the best."

"That's you."

Daniella shook her head. "I'll never be able to make him believe that. I'm not sure I believe it."

Trenton drove up to the stately Victorian mansion and parked. Cars spilled out the driveway; perhaps they were hosting a party. But Daniella's roommate hadn't mentioned that. He turned to Layla. "This won't take long." He took her leash and walked toward the house. He stopped when he saw a beautiful little girl come from around the back. Her eyes widened when she saw him and he heard her gasp with delight before she burst into a run—toward them. He squatted to her level, thinking that Layla had caught her interest, but instead she ran to him and hugged him.

"Well, hello there," he said, hiding his surprise.

"My name is Kati. Is this your dog?"

"Yes."

"We have a cat, but my Aunty Mari has two dogs and one is really big."

"Would you like to pet her?"

She nodded. "She's so pretty."

"So are you."

She giggled. "I know that."

He laughed. "That's good." He glanced up and saw

two men coming around the corner. One was an older man with a limp, the other in dusty jeans. Trenton quickly stood then realized he was still holding the little girl and put her down. "Hi, I was just—" He tapped his chest. "She came up to me."

They stared at him, amazed, as if he'd just turned purple and grown antlers.

He held out his hand, not understanding their reaction. "I'm Trenton Sheppard."

They didn't move. "I've never seen her do that before," one of the men said. "She'd usually shy of strangers, especially men. If I hadn't seen it for myself I wouldn't have believed it."

Trenton let his hand fall to his side. "For some reason kids like me."

"I see. I'm Alex and this is my friend Tony. You've already met my daughter. I know you're here to see Daniella."

Trenton nodded. "Yes."

"Look, she's young and kind and that Pascal guy used her so if you're here to berate her I'm not going to allow it."

"I'm not here for that. I just want to talk to her, but I see you have company."

"Her sisters are here. You'll get used to it. They're very close."

"You sound confident that I'll win her over."

Alex laughed. "After seeing what you can do to Kati, I'm convinced."

Trenton sighed. "I'm afraid I haven't been as lucky with women as I've been with kids."

Kati jumped up and down, clapping her hands. "Can I show you my dollhouse?" She took Trenton's hand.

"Uh…sure," Trenton said as Kati tried to lead him away.

"Actually that's a good idea," Alex said. "I'll get Daniella and meet you around the back. Tony, go with them."

Alex went inside the house and motioned to his wife.

"What is it?" she said.

He took her hand and led her to the back garden. "You've got to see this." He took her to the back window and pointed while Kati sat on Trenton's lap and put a pink boa around his neck.

"Who is that?"

"Trenton."

"Daniella's Trenton?"

"Yes, and Kati ran to him as if she'd known him for years."

"He's very patient with her."

"Poor man, we should save him. I'll go get Dani."

Unlike her sister, Daniella wasn't surprised by the sight that met her when she went out into the garden.

"When you're with children and animals I see your parents in you."

He turned and stood. "Hi."

"I'm so sorry. I shouldn't have trusted Pascal."

"I'm not here to talk about that." He held out two slips of paper. "You forgot these."

She took them.

"Layla came to say thank you."

"And you?"

"I'm sorry I even doubted you for a minute. It won't happen again."

"I'm glad."

"I have a question I want to ask you but I'm not sure I have the right to when I have so little to offer you right now, but if you're willing to wait—"

"I'm not."

His face fell. "Okay, I understand."

"I can't wait. I want to marry you."

"It's not going to be easy. I still have an uphill battle ahead of me."

"And I'll be right by your side."

He kissed her. "I'd hoped you'd say that."

Daniella took his hand with the same eagerness Kati did moments ago. "Now it's time for you to meet everyone."

Everyone welcomed him as if he'd already become one of the family.

"You know there's a penalty for marrying into this family," Alex said loud enough for others to hear.

"What?"

"Getting Mariella as a sister-in-law."

Mariella sauntered past him like a tigress. "Neanderthal," she said.

"Snow Queen," he shot back.

"She's harmless," Tony said.

"She's a beautiful woman," Trenton admitted. "But she looks anything but harmless. Has anyone taken up the challenge?"

"I have," a dark voice said behind them.

They turned to the tall man dressed in black. Alex

smiled, patting the newcomer on the back. "Ian, you're just in time." He jerked his thumb in Trenton's direction. "We're welcoming Trenton into the family."

Ian shifted his dark gaze to Trenton. "Sounds to me like you were giving him a warning."

"I thought it's only fair. Most men aren't as brave as you."

Isabella playfully pinched her husband. "Behave yourself, Lex. We don't want to scare him away."

Daniella wrapped her arms around Trenton in a loving embrace. "You can't. Nothing can scare him away." She looked into his eyes seeing not only the man she adored, but the man she wanted to spend her life with. "He's my hero."

Trenton tenderly kissed her and smiled, feeling a sense of home and a hope for a bright future with a family of his own, that he hadn't felt in a long time. "And I'm here to stay."

Epilogue

Three years later

"Stop squirming! If you don't sit still, I'll burn you."

Daniella froze, biting back a sharp reply as her sister Mariella parted and started curling a strand of her hair with a hot curling iron.

It was her wedding day and it had been four hours since she'd awoken at 5:30 a.m. to get ready. The makeup artist had come and gone, leaving Mariella to style her hair. Daniella secretly regretted not going to the salon as planned, but her sister had convinced her that she could save time and money by doing it herself. "So much for saving time," Daniella mumbled, stealing a glance at the clock on the far wall.

"Beauty takes time," Mariella said, unfazed by her sister's grim tone. "I just need to add some attachments."

She reached for a braided bun with burgundy highlights, and attached it to the back of Daniella's hair, holding the elaborate upswept design in place with two twenty-four-carat-gold hair combs. "There. Finished." Mariella sighed and rested her perfectly manicured hand on her chest, evidently pleased with herself. "God, I'm good."

"Shouldn't I be the judge of that?"

Mariella shrugged. "You'll agree."

Daniella started to turn to look at herself in the mirror, but Mariella stopped her. "No." She grabbed her sister's arm, pulled her out of the chair and led her to the full-length mirror. "You have to see what Trenton will."

Daniella started to, but Isabella burst into the room before she had a chance. "Are you done yet? We only have two hours before the limousine arrives and…" Her voice fell away as she stared at her youngest sister. "Oh, you look exquisite."

Mariella beamed, fanning herself with her hand. "I told you I was good."

Isabella and Daniella shared a look then Daniella shifted her gaze to look at herself. She gasped, hardly recognizing herself in the off-the-shoulder, A-line white satin gown with hand-beaded bodice and a gorgeous silk train. She was amazed that this day had finally come when it had seemed so far out of reach only months earlier.

She'd found Trenton sitting on the balcony of their one-bedroom apartment staring at the setting sun. They'd moved to Philadelphia to be closer to his parents and had had to depend on their financial support when Trenton decided to sue Brooks's estate for damages, loss and mental anguish due to his conviction, which was subsequently overturned. They hadn't expected the battle to take three years. He had a tense, quiet energy as he stared out at the horizon.

Daniella took a hesitant step toward him. "What's wrong?"

He didn't turn, his gaze transfixed by the liquid gold sweeping across the office buildings in the distance. "I've waited over three years for this."

She gripped her hand into a fist. "What?"

He grabbed her wrist and pulled her onto his lap. "It's over. Miller just called. He found Brooks's three offshore accounts, which total over thirteen million dollars. Half of that will be part of my settlement."

Travis Miller was Trenton's lawyer and he'd hired a private detective to find out about Brooks's accounts. He'd claimed bankruptcy and financial hardship. Miller had also worked with Brooks's now ex-wife, Fayola, who had married a French diplomat and moved to the Cayman Islands, and helped lead him to some of Brooks's hidden assets.

Daniella threw her arms around Trenton's neck and hugged him, thrilled to see the shadow of stress and strain leave his eyes. "That's wonderful. Want to celebrate?"

He shook his head. "No."

She straightened and stared at him. "Oh, you want to call your parents first?" she asked, eager to share the good news.

Trenton wrapped his arms around her waist before she could stand. "No. I don't want to do that either. At least not yet." He took a deep breath. "I didn't expect this day to take three years, but…" He reached into his trouser pocket and pulled out a small jewelry box. "Daniella Duvall, will you marry me again?"

"Again?"

"Yes." He took her hand and slid off the small ring he'd placed on her finger when they'd gone to the justice of the peace two years earlier. He replaced it with a larger stone. "I want to give you the wedding you deserve. The wedding you've always dreamed of."

Six months later he fulfilled that promise.

Daniella took Ian's arm and stepped into the main ballroom of the Rosewood Hotel, a massive structure designed like a Tuscan villa. No detail was missed from the lavish chandeliers overhead and gorgeous bouquets of red roses that lined the aisle, to the plush white carpet leading her to her groom. As a string quartet played the "Wedding March," the assembled guests stood and turned to look at her.

Trenton looked at her and stared, wondering if he'd ever be able to breathe again. The sight of her left him breathless. Only three years ago, his life was in shambles, he had no money, no career, and now he was starting a new life with a woman who had changed it in more ways than he could fathom. She had supported his decision to sue Brooks. She had stood beside him during the trial, standing by his side every step of the way. When they received the final settlement, she encouraged him to get recertified as a medic pilot and go into business with Duane to open a world-class search-and-rescue training program. She'd become not only an essential part of his life, but of him. As long as he lived, he knew his heart would beat in tune to hers.

Suddenly she stood beside him, and he took her hand and winked. "Is this all that you'd hoped for, Ginger?"

Daniella broke into a wide open smile, making his heart sing at the thought of the years he got to spend loving her. "Yes, Professor. You've made all my dreams come true."

* * * * *

REQUEST YOUR FREE BOOKS!

2 FREE NOVELS
PLUS 2 FREE GIFTS!

KIMANI ROMANCE ™

Love's ultimate destination!